THE SLEEPING CAR PORTER

THE SLEEPING CAR PORTER

SUZETTE MAYR

COACH HOUSE BOOKS, TORONTO

first edition

Published with the generous assistance of the Canada Council for the Arts and the Ontario Arts Council. Coach House Books also acknowledges the support of the Government of Canada through the Canada Book Fund and the Government of Ontario through the Ontario Book Publishing Tax Credit.

LIBRARY AND ARCHIVES CANADA CATALOGUING IN PUBLICATION

Title: The sleeping car porter / Suzette Mayr.
Names: Mayr, Suzette, author.
Identifiers: Canadiana (print) 2022019937X | Canadiana (ebook) 20220199388 | ISBN 9781552454589 (softcover) | ISBN 9781770567269 (EPUB) | ISBN 9781770567276 (PDF)
Classification: LCC PS8576.A9 S54 2022 | DDC C813/.54—dc23
Printed in Canada

The Sleeping Car Porter is available as an ebook: ISBN 978 1 77056 726 9 (EPUB), ISBN 978 1 77056 727 6 (PDF)

Purchase of the print version of this book entitles you to a free digital copy. To claim your ebook of this title, please email sales@chbooks.com with proof of purchase. (Coach House Books reserves the right to terminate the free digital download offer at any time.)

For Don Bragg
and for Davis

I loved my friend.
He went away from me.
There's nothing more to say.
The poem ends,
Soft as it began –
I loved my friend.

– 'Poem (For F. S.),' Langston Hughes, 1925

As the train pulls into a station in the early evening
darkness you disappear.

– *Waiting for Saskatchewan*, Fred Wah, 1985

BEFORE

9:45 p.m. Standing next to his step box, Baxter hovers: immobile and elastic, ready to spring forward to lift a suitcase, dissect a timetable, point to the conductor, nod, lift more suitcases, now hat boxes, answer more questions, and nod, nod, nod. Trouser cuffs drag in the dust, shiny boot heels clap against the train-station platform; a child runs toward an observation car, ribbons and cufflinks and tickets and goodbye letters swish to the ground. Hands reach toward him, grab at him for a lift up, grab his coat pocket, wave in his face. A sea swell of passengers, spilling toward his car; a maelstrom of departure-time panic.

R.T. Baxter, dentist-to-be, man who longs to lance gums and extract pathological third molars, standing, here, next to this train, caught in this hurricane.

Drowsy already.

Boarding Baxter's train car, pushing past a mother squeezing the elbows of her tot, a man shaped like a heart, shaped like a mango, pauses on the step box before alighting into the car. Mango hooks his index finger in the air, parts his dry lips, but no sound, no question mark comes out.

– You're in Compartment C, sir, says Baxter, even though the conductor just told that to the passenger. Baxter's not sure what more the passenger might want to know right now, or what the silent, hooked finger might mean. – Welcome aboard, says Baxter.

– Midnight, Mango says. Then he slips the finger into a breast pocket and slides out a business card. He flips the card to Baxter. The profession says *Optician*. On the back the passenger has printed in tiny letters:

Midnight. Not a minute later.

The card's sharp corners jab Baxter's fingertips. Baxter will still be coaxing passengers to settle into their berths at midnight, he'll be tripping over pillows and pyjamas at midnight. He has a shadowy idea about what the man's tiny and precise lettering means, but passengers can also be shifty creatures, affably baring their teeth one moment but in the next doing so wickedly. Baxter has no time to play a personal Dorothy Dix and listen to Mango's nighttime confessions about a mouldering love affair or a profligate brother during the time Baxter needs to black boots and fill out reports. Passengers will still be toppling around drunk or ringing at him for the ladder, or meandering back and forth to the toilet, back and forth, pestering him to ask, *When will the train pass through Octopus?* or *Why has the train slowed down?*, as if he rides on top of the train when he's out of their sight. Maybe Mango the Optician can scoop out Baxter's human eyes and pop owl telescope eyes into Baxter's eye sockets instead.

Feathers drift before Baxter's eyes. He blinks them away, rubs his glasses with a handkerchief. Not feathers. Hardly any sleep last night, no sleep for two nights on the run before this, and now his eyeballs are fogging up. He slides the optician's card into his breast pocket.

Baxter fills out reports and heaves boxes up and down and up, trips over pillows and pyjamas as he checks every berth, every compartment, notes who needs their shoes polished and who's already been drinking so hard they'll never find their way down the very straight, very narrow passageway.

At 11:59 p.m., Baxter presses the pearly doorbell to Compartment C. Mango opens the door, a cigar smouldering in his mouth, the smoke and the smell in the compartment smashing through the doorway, the shoulders on his top-heavy body filling the doorway.

– Right on time, says Mango, smoke puffing with each word.

He jabs a five-dollar bill at Baxter, and Baxter reaches for it, dizzy at the gargantuan amount of money. Mango jerks it back and rips it in two; he offers one half to Baxter and winks, his lips sneering around the cigar. Time lashes to a stop. Mango is one of those nasty types, one who wants Baxter as an alibi or witness for some stupid or terrible thing he hasn't done yet but he knows he's going to do. Baxter folds the half bill in two, slides its foulness into his uniform breast pocket.

Baxter remembers that mangos have big, obtrusive pits.

– The other half at the end of the trip, Mango murmurs to Baxter, and claps Baxter on the shoulder.

Long hairs prickle out of the passenger's nostrils, his ear holes. Baxter's seen men like him before. He's not seen them too. His Porter Instructor Edwin Drew told him all about men like this. *Love Diplomats*, he called them.

– Here, Mango says. – You forgot these.

He shoves a pair of shoes at Baxter, their insides moist and stinking. Then he shuts the compartment door, banging it into Baxter's toe.

Baxter tucks more passengers into their beds, wipes up water splashed around the washbasins; he fetches extra towels. His twin reflection bustles in white-jacketed circles in the mirrors, sweat droplets pocking its forehead, its face long and thin, eyeglasses glinting. The second hour of a nearly forty-eight-hour run, and he already wants to curl up and blow away.

Baxter knocks dirt from the soles of Mango's shoes, swipes his brush back and forth on the toes, on the heels, along the sides. Dabs and rubs shoeshine paste and water into the toes, rubs with a rag until the leather gleams. The shoe leather stiff and bright. Baxter taps his fingers along the ornate stitching and broguing, for just a moment.

Stinkpot.

He slides the shoes into the tiny locker beside Mango's door. He sits back down on his stool and shines other passengers' shoes and boots, his fingernails grubby with paste, shining his way into the flattest part of the night when he can pack up his shoeshine kit, when he can set up his *own* bed, when even the fussiest of passengers are dreaming past their need to ring for a porter.

Still, every so often the bell on his call board summons him, and he moves the ladder to an upper berth so a passenger can descend for a midnight visit to the lavatory or other hijinks. Or climb up like a drunk, sleepy squirrel.

The night slides by outside the train windows, the rocking and swaying of the car. Baxter rubs his eyes so hard that aurorae borealis undulate inside his eyelids.

At 2:00 a.m., in the smoker compartment next to the WC, he pulls out a sliver-thin mattress and fits it on top of the sofa. He stretches out on the mattress, his head sagging sideways into sleep. His fingers scrabble for a sheet to pull up to his neck, then his fingers remember he forgot to put on a sheet. He also forgot to ask the porter in the next car to cover for him. He needs to stand up, he needs to straighten up. He plummets backward into sleep.

The bell clangs him awake after only twenty minutes. He totters to his feet.

A late-night tomcat wearing nothing but pyjamas and a trench coat staggers intoxicated up into one of the empty upper berths while Baxter grips the ladder steady. The tomcat was trying to scramble up into his upper berth by himself, stepping and kicking all over the lower berth. The man in the lower pressed the bell to call Baxter, then burrowed himself back in.

– Thank you very very verrrrrrry mush, whispers the drunk, pulling the blanket up to his armpits. – Porter, he hisses, – Porter! Looka this. Looka what I got.

Mr. Liquor Head props himself up on an elbow. He rustles inside his pyjama pocket and pulls out a tattered, much-thumbed postcard and slides it to Baxter. – Hee hee, he giggles.

Baxter peers at the card through the dim.

Two women, clothed in nothing but stockings, flopped together on a chesterfield.

– Got it from France, says Liquor Head. – *Paris.*

Baxter smooths the ragged, smutty card on the edge of the mattress. Sweat slithers out on his forehead, on the back of his neck. One lady's white teeth line her lips like tiny flower petals.

He hovers here, perched on the ladder's bottom step, as he frantically grubs in his head for what he can pretend. He can't pretend interest. Not even for the biggest tip in the world. He doesn't want to get fired or beaten to death for leering at a naked white lady, and he doesn't want to earn demerit points for *undue familiarity* with this passenger. He can't pretend nausea. No, that wouldn't do.

Liquor Head frowns, huffs his disapproval when Baxter doesn't whistle or titter at the smutty outrageousness of the card, huffs his annoyance because Baxter so far registers nothing at all.

Liquor Head grabs back his postcard, the irritation igniting his face.

Baxter flips into funny and charming. Just like Edwin Drew.

– Looks like their husbands forgot to buy them coats, says Baxter.

Liquor Head sniffles a laugh through his nose and throws his head backwards onto his pillow.

Baxter erupts in a silent, dizzy, exhausted, steam-engine hoot. It's very, very funny imagining the kind of lady who would marry a snaggle-toothed fellow like this passenger, whose hand clawing the postcard sports a wedding ring. Baxter doesn't even begin to know how a real dentist would diagnose the tangle of teeth in the man's mouth, possibly a result of delayed eruption of the permanent teeth or abnormal roots.

– Sir, says Baxter, – you have a good night now, sir.

The man chirps a giggle.

Clean up after yourself, thinks Baxter.

He gently shakes the berth curtain for a passenger who's due to detrain, three in the morning.

– Morning, says the passenger, pawing crusts from his eyes. – Does 3:00 a.m. count as morning?

Baxter's lips won't let him answer. Sleepiness clouds his head too.

The passenger pokes his feet out from his berth, then rolls to the floor in the aisle, woozy from the eerie hour.

Baxter almost has to carry him and his suitcase out the door and down to the step box on the platform, Baxter's hand subtly curled for coins or maybe a bill. Rolly, the porter in the car after Baxter's, helps down a passenger who accidentally spills a shower of coins. Rolly hunts for the rolling coins in the dark of the platform, shaking his head, his platter-sized hands patting the ground before they catch up to the silver.

Baxter's passenger presses twenty-five cents into Baxter's palm. That's fine. Not remarkable. Only fine. Enough for a fancy toothbrush, but not significant enough to bump up Baxter's dentistry school fund.

Baxter rolls up the soiled sheets crumpled in the empty berth. His bell rings. He draws water for a passenger who snaps her fingers at him. Baxter retrieves the emptied cup one minute later, its edges dewy. He crosses the vestibule between his car and the next, pauses as the door to the next car stretches up like rubber so it's ten feet high, then bounces back down again. He closes his eyes for a nap the size of a poppy seed, then pulls open the door. Rolly is whisking a feather duster along the walls in the passageway. Baxter taps Rolly on the shoulder. Rolly drops the duster.

– Cheese and bread! exclaims Rolly, bending and chasing the duster as it rolls away, the ostrich feathers flicking as it rolls. – Don't creep up on a man like that.

– I need to go down, Baxter says.

– I was going to ask you! says Rolly. – Soon as I was finished dusting!

– Can you watch my car? asks Baxter.

A freight train rattles by, drenching them in sound. Rolly's lips curl and clench as he retorts, showing only the row of lower incisors as he complains and waves his duster in his giant beanstalk hands. Baxter can't hear him and smiles sweet as a plum.

They connect their car bells so that when Baxter's bell rings, Rolly has to jump.

– Rest in peace, says Rolly, running his sausage fingers along a lintel. He holds up a finger, trailing a cobweb, and points it in Baxter's face.

Baxter coils onto his side on the mattress, on the sofa, the mattress so narrow he nearly rolls off with each lurch of the car. His eyelids padlock shut.

A passenger slams the WC door.

Baxter's eyelids splinter apart. He lurches up to sitting. His stomach burbles with hunger so he peels the wrapping off a sandwich in his bag. He dozes off. Opens his eyes again, the sandwich flopped in his hands. He gnaws at the crust, so tired he can't even tell what kind of sandwich he's chewing, shreds of grey meat between his teeth, dissolving on his tongue, dulled into nothing. His tongue and teeth remember his aunt Arimenta's stew fish and grits, fresh from the sea just a few streets away, fresh from the pot, steaming on his plate. Her slim hips as she stood at the stove stirring the pot, her veined hands reloading his plate every time he emptied it. Back and forth. She herself ate only one meal a day to stay trim, she said. – Save a little money too, she said.

She smoked her pipe while he and his cousins ate.

The train whistle shrieks.

He clamps his teeth into the papery sandwich over and over because his time has run out. 7:00 a.m. He guzzles blood-warm milk from a bottle as the sun froths up over the horizon. He tucks away the bottle. He unhooks the extension cord connecting the car bells, Rolly so engrossed in writing a letter to a lady friend he barely nods hello. Passengers wobble awake, and Baxter gulps down the last shards of sandwich.

8:00 a.m. Baxter heaves berths closed. He gathers up stray apple cores, glasses cases, fallen collars, and pins. He wipes down nickel-plated basins, woodwork clouded from hands and faces. 11:00 a.m., he fetches bags, hat boxes, Scotch Mints, a peach.

Then afternoon. He tucks away, he picks up, he fetches, he spins a story. He sits in an empty section, his torso rocking with the movement of the train, his fingers tapping the plush upholstery. He sits and sits and sits, punching away sleep while passengers ooze hot air, while they flip pages of mystery books, point out the windows at stony forests, daisies sprouting in ditches, jersey cows dotting fields. He doesn't remember falling asleep, he could lose his job if he falls asleep during the day, but he must have closed his eyes for a second too long because he nods awake, and a dried fig of a passenger in an adjoining section rustles his *Beaver* magazine at Baxter. Did he snore? Did he miss a passenger wanting a safety pin? He strides back to the smoker to check the call board, but all the arrows point straight. He sits in the smoker, holding up his eyelids with his thumbs. The thin layer of smoke haze in the room froths, clots into storm clouds cracking with needles of lightning. No it doesn't.

The bell rings. Lower 4.

– I want a Coca-Cola, says the passenger in Lower 4. – My gout's flared up, you see, and it's too far to walk.

– Yes, sir.

Baxter squeezes down passageways through car after car until he reaches the club car.

He squeezes back.

Lower 4 holds out his hand for the glass without looking at Baxter, dips a top lip into the glass and sips.

The flannel-suited passenger across the aisle leans toward Baxter.

– That Coca-Cola looks just fine, says Flannel, eyeing the Coca-Cola. – Hmm. A cup of tea in my hand would be very nice right now, he says, looking out the window at a bog, at a rickety little bridge collapsed in the bog.

The passenger wants tea?

Flannel spins his head to Baxter.

– *A cup of tea in my hand would be very nice right now*, Flannel says, snapping his fingers.

Baxter sucks in air through his nostrils, then spews it out his mouth. – Yes, sir, he says.

Flannel leans back into the flowery fabric upholstering his seat and folds his hands over his flannelly stomach. The skipping light between the trees mirrors in Flannel's face, in each insectival eye of Flannel's round, glossy eyeglasses.

Baxter fetches and delivers the tea, the thick steam winding up into his nostrils, so balmy after the tepid half bottle of milk this morning. He drags out a suitcase so a passenger can retrieve a book, chases after a child's bright rubber ball as it escapes into a vestibule, crumples a handkerchief dropped out of someone's pocket. He tells a story he makes up on the spot because someone with a fancy watch on his wrist demands it about a mountain explorer who fell headfirst into a crevasse in a Rocky Mountain glacier and, while wedged upside down, glimpsed a winged man frozen in the ice.

All this time, the train glides over its gleaming tracks between Pakesley, Westree, Gogama, and Agate, between trees and rocks and over flatland, more rock, over ancient stories.

Even when he stands still, he moves. Baxter flickers everywhere and nowhere. A blink in a shuddering train window.

He would love to catapult off the train the vile man who cusses at him for spilling coffee in the man's lap even though the man, with his bloodshot eyes and halitosis, spilled the coffee himself, the cup and saucer tinkling in his shaky hands. Baxter would like to sock him right on the nose. The passenger's upper and lower teeth interact abnormally as he snarls and speckles spit, revealing what Baxter surmises is an overbite, a malocclusion to be precise, as well as a missing posterior tooth, perhaps a first molar, the man's swearing too quickly for Baxter to be sure. The deteriorating enamel on the teeth of an American who drank too many Canadian Clubs in the club car last night and chewed too much tobacco every other night, the train rolling and rumbling its disapproval as the man leaps to his feet then falls right back down into his seat again because of his unsteady legs, the car's perpetual motion. If only the man would hold his snout open long enough so Baxter could poke his fingers at what also looks to be apparent abrasion or attrition of his teeth as a result of friction between the surfaces of his opposing teeth. Blood washes out of the man's face and his lips clamp shut mid-swear, so Baxter helps the man to the WC, the two of them squishing down the passageway like toothpaste in a tube, then Baxter has to mop up the vomitous mess because the dope disgorged everywhere but down the hopper. Baxter gags. Swallows back the gag.

Baxter apologizes for the spilled coffee. When he gets off the train in Winnipeg, he doesn't want the rotten surprise of being called upstairs and given more demerits, or the giant blade that hangs suspended over every porter: fired for some small deed he did or didn't do, like not grovelling enough in his apology to a passenger who's spilled coffee on himself. And that other young fellow he worked with for two days, James, who had fifty-eight demerits, then at the end of his run in Montreal learned he'd exceeded the maximum sixty demerits, so *God be with you*, said the company. James's *services* were *dispensed with*, as the *Instructions* book so neatly puts it.

James was given demerits and fired for stepping on an upholstered seat arm while he was making up an upper berth. Then he was fired again for not apologizing when a passenger called him *George* and James corrected the passenger, the horse's back snapping in half from that final feather when that passenger called him *George*. His name wasn't George, it was James Alfred Marshall Clutterbuck, Thanking you, *sir!*

The train chugs and clatters its way to Longlac. The sun slinks away, the dark night floods in. The train squeals into Longlac. Pulls away again. Baxter balls up soiled sheets, doles out more pillows.

12:45 a.m., Mango from Compartment C totters drunk though the car, lurches from side to side, slapping the walls as they prop him up. His feet stutter, and he tips forward.

Baxter leaps up and clutches Mango by the elbow.

– SSSHHH … Mango pats Baxter's hand. – I think I'm lost.

– I'll help you to your compartment, whispers Baxter.

– Yessss, says Mango. – That would be very gallant of you.

He stumbles.

– Yes, that would be swell.

He pats his hands along the walls and railings, the wainscoting. His fingers smear trails of sweat over the gleaming trim.

– Here we go, announces Baxter.

– Thank you, says Mango, patting Baxter's solar plexus. – A pleasure to make your acquaintance.

He holds out his hand to shake, his leer exposing teeth crusted with excessive calculus and swollen redness on the inside of his bottom lip and inside his cheek: the man likely suffers from follicular stomatitis from too much cigar-smoking. Fascinating. Baxter keeps his face blank, his repulsion at Mango's touch even blanker as he shakes Mango's hot, knuckly hand.

Mango yanks Baxter in and lands his mouth on Baxter's mouth in a calculus-caked, stomatitis kiss.

Baxter thrusts him away and shoves Mango back into the plush of his compartment. Wipes his mouth with the back of his hand.

– Yooop! says Mango as he crashes into his berth. – *Yearning … just for yoooooou*, he sings, and he scissors open his arms to Baxter.

Baxter's chest crackles as Mango pulls out the other torn half of the five-dollar bill, the tip of his tongue clamped between his upper and lower incisors, a pink worm.

Baxter shuts the door.

From inside the compartment, Mango bumps around, then there's a thump.

Baxter wipes the back of his shaking hand on his thigh. Wipes his mouth again with what he thinks is his handkerchief but is instead a cleaning rag he stuffs back into his pocket. The taste of expensive spirits, dust, and cobweb ghosts his lips. The half five-dollar bill festers deep in his pocket where he thrust it, and the other half of that bill dangles on the other side of this door. Baxter will report Mango to the conductor. Yes, he will!

Five dollars would pay rent for a room for at least two weeks. It would make a locomotive-sized deposit into his dentistry school fund.

Mango will report him for some phantasmic crime; Baxter will lose this job and linger out the rest of his life shining shoes on street corners, chasing dropped pennies and shiny buttons.

He stumbles to the vestibule and crouches down in a corner. He rubs his forehead with his palms back and forth, back and forth, his forehead wet then wetter.

He whips the rag out of his pocket, slams open the door back to the passageway, and begins rubbing brass rails, polishing them as hard as he can until they shine in pain.

Rolly asks him to watch his car.

Shoes and boots, Baxter needs to gather and shine shoes and black boots. This lousy run. Twenty more hours. Two cars.

He sits on his stool by his bell. His eyes are as dry as raisins. For hours, for hours and hours.

Rolly, yawning wildly from his too-short sleep, spells him off.

Baxter lies down on the sofa in the smoker. The WC door slams back and forth, the sound crashing his body awake every single time.

Mango is scheduled to detrain at 7:15 a.m. in Fort William, breakfast at 6:00 a.m. At 5:45 a.m., Baxter presses the buzzer to Compartment C. Knocks.

Nothing.

Knocks.

Baxter eases his backside onto his stool.

Compartment C's bell rings.

Baxter opens the compartment door to Mango, disintegrated in his berth. A sweater swaddles his head, with only his nose poking out.

– *Waw... der*, he croaks.

The window blind stays drawn in the compartment as Baxter steadies a cup of water in Mango's pickled hands, a split cigar wedged between two of Mango's fingers. Rheum spiders Mango's eyelids, and saliva has dried trails in the corners of his mouth.

– Here you go, says Baxter. – *Sir.*

Mango mumbles, – *Brain… split.*

The train heaves into Fort William at 7:14 a.m., and passengers totter, skip, and waddle down the steps and onto his step box. Baxter holds his hand out. Subtle. His palm shaped like the bowl of a shallow spoon so no coins can roll out. He smiles wide, but not too wide. He doesn't want to look like he's got a *grin.*

Some passengers tip with a flourish, some as though change and bills are contraband goods. Baxter's pocket jingles with pennies and nickels.

Mango descends the stairs. His face is watery, his eyes squinty and red-veined from his hangover. He hovers groggily at the top of the steps, as though he might tumble down them, his shoes gleaming from Baxter's shining.

Yearning just for yooooooou.

Mango stumbles down.

– See ya later, boy, he says, not tipping at all.

Baxter nods and curls his lips up, automaton-happy, just in case a spotter's watching. Maybe Mango *was* a spotter!

The train sweeps away from Fort William, away from Mango the duplicitous optician. Speeds through Upsala, Wabigoon, Cloverleaf. Lurches into Winnipeg 9:15 p.m., and Baxter sets out his step box. He whisks tiny bits of cinder, soot, and dust, visible and invisible, off passenger shoulders as they step off the train; he brushes off their hats; he holds out his arm if they tilt. He says a last name he spies on a passenger's suitcase to flatter the passenger into thinking he's more important than the King of Siam. He holds out his hand. Subtle. Like Edwin Drew taught him.

Tips: $6.47 total from Toronto to Winnipeg. Not so bad. And Mango's crummy half bill.

When he's stumbled to the top of the steps at headquarters, he's told he's getting five demerits.

Five!

– But why? he asks.

He sets his satchel and shoeshine kit on the wood floor and irons his face flat as he waits for the fabulation Mango made up.

– Coffee stain on your shirt.

Baxter wants to swear and shout and burn down the station with fiery flashes of light.

– But a *passenger* spilled the coffee on me, he says.

– Tell it to the Marines.

He's now collected fifty demerits. The superintendent mentions nothing about Mango.

Baxter supposes he should be grateful he still has his job, but really he wants to hunker down and cry.

He kicks his way into a jagged half sleep at a boarding house near the station. Not that he can ever sleep when lying in a *proper* bed. In the morning, he trades fifteen cents for a new toothbrush to cheer himself up. He pops the brush into his mouth and chews the bristles.

Then he's stuck riding an empty car back east – not enough passengers have booked for this run – but he still sits kitted out in his monkey suit, stupid and stiff, just in case. Tips: $0 and 0¢ total. He turns over and over a prickly ball of frustration. Fifty demerits. Only ten to go. The railyards outside the window flip past, brick houses, weeds, rubbish, rickety shacks. He dozes, but jolts awake with the buzz of his own snoring. He tugs out of his satchel an issue of *Weird Tales* he found two runs ago. He takes great gulps of the magazine: A story about a Robot who murders. A jellyfish who digests a professor.

He pretends the train snakes on the surface of the planet Mars.

He tries to doze, perhaps even sleep, but the five new demerits keep cutting him awake. His magazine milked dry, he fishes a book out of his satchel. *The Scarab from Jupiter*. Oh, it's capital!

In Toronto, he hops a train to Montreal. On his *own* time.

Baxter spends the single day strolling among the buildings of McGill University. His goal: McGill Dental School. Starting September 1931. He's been saving for eight years, and in only two more years, in 1931, if he stays on track, he will have $1,068 saved, enough for four years of dentistry school. Right now he has $967 saved. $101 to go. He can porter in the summers for the room and board. He will figure out how to afford the instruments even if it means not eating. He will find instruments somehow. He found an abandoned dentistry textbook on a train eight years ago: *The Practice of Dentistry: A Practical Treatise upon the General Practice of Dentistry, Operative and Prosthetic, Exclusive of Orthodontic Practice*. He began reading it, and even before he reached the end of the first chapter on the eruption of deciduous teeth, a bonfire blazed inside him.

At 7:00 p.m. he parks his bag and his shoeshine kit at a house near the Windsor train station in Montreal that's friendly to porters. He lays his head down on his pillow at 8:00 p.m., hoping sleep will track him down.

After two hours, he wakes up and tosses himself from his belly to his back to his side. Flops back onto his stomach again, wide awake, dreading the sun as it plots its inevitable rise. He starts sliding into a dream about a beetle paddling in a pot of stew, when the landlady and her missing mandibular right premolar scream because she's dropped a hot pan of potatoes, and her husband the retired porter with a chipped cuspid starts shouting, *You'll wake! Everyone! Up!*

He could sleep for fifty-two hours, at least. He's twenty-nine years old, but his bones, his joints, rattle like he's edging into his 189th birthday.

He reports back at the yards for station duty in the morning, which means he may get a run. Or he may just spend the day at the station waiting for a run that never appears. Yawning and tripping over ties while cars and locomotives shunt, wheeze, and clank back and forth, because he is an extra and it is his job to stand around and take the runs he's told to take. A porter's wife hurries into the office with her hair stuffed up under a ribbony hat – her husband's sick from pneumonia and can't show up to his Montreal–Vancouver line tonight, so Baxter of course says yes, like he has any choice, even though the trip is three days and four nights one way. And no surety of a return run. Learning about malocclusions and impacted molars requires money. Baxter will sleep briefly, more of a nap, no matter how droopy-eyed he gets. He's a sleepy car porter. Ha ha. That's a dandy!

He has to wait before he can board his car. He takes a piss in the toilets at the bottom of a hotel near the train station. A white man settles into the urinal right next to Baxter's, his arms thick under his shirt sleeves.

– Evening, says the man, pissing. He stops. Shakes it out. Shakes it out for far longer than necessary.

Baxter pauses, his fly open. He considers the man's thick, strong arms. He considers where he and the man are for a moment, and where they could go. But the man stands far too straight and soldierly in the shoulders, and this troubles him.

Baxter buttons up his trousers and walks away.

A  B

DAY ONE
(MONTREAL TO SUDBURY)

He dwindles the day away reading *The Scarab from Jupiter*, trailing the six Egyptologists as they blunder into the wrong mummy's tomb. His heart starts pattering quickly because the golden beetles have skittered into their bags of tools, and one has crawled up the trouser leg of the head Egyptologist. That's a terrible development. Baxter gulps water from his bottle and eats one cold beef and then two sardine sandwiches, one right after the other, in a patch of weeds outside the railyards. He has a sausage in a bun from the landlady tucked in his bag for later.

He wanted to go to the best chicken house he knew, where all the porters liked to eat, and stuff food into himself until he couldn't breathe because the food on the train would be nothing but expensive, burned crusts scraped from the bottoms of the pots and the station lunch counters probably few and far between. But he saw another porter, Eugene Grady, up ahead of him, sucking hard on a cigarette and hauling open the door to the restaurant in his theatrical way, as though every room, every building, was his stage, to the boisterous hellos of a crew of men already inside, Eugene's straw sailor set back far on his head, ready to squabble, so Baxter ducked away.

Eugene is Edwin Drew's brother-in-law.

Edwin Drew. Baxter's Porter Instructor from years ago.

Eugene also likes far too much to make fun of Baxter's love for scientifiction, which makes Baxter want to bite the insides of his cheeks off.

Sandwiches chewed and piled up inside his stomach, Baxter stands among the stone arches decorating the train station, trying to sew a loose button on his jacket while waiting for the run to start, but a policeman taps him hard on the shoulder.

The policeman's belly sticks out under his uniform, the man well fed, his teeth small ice chips.

– Move it or I'll get you for loitering.

Baxter stuffs his needle and thread in his pocket and starts walking. Loitering! Why would he want to loiter in a train station if he didn't have to? He had his fill of locomotives' hissing and screams long ago, had tired of their whistly spurts and steam farting the first day he started. The railyard smell always jerks his stomach, sometimes telling him he still hasn't eaten enough and his stomach is too soft.

It reminds him of his mother accusing him of too much daydreaming, as though daydreaming was a crime because it sometimes made him late for school. Yes, perhaps he daydreamed too much, talked to stray dogs and geckos, trying to make them his friends, dithered over his fish at breakfast, drew pictures of the stars at bedtime.

He flees the stone arches, steps up onto curbs, then back down again, hops over plops of horse manure as he toddles the blocks around the station trying to look as though he's walking somewhere, not *loitering*. He's *supposed* to linger at the station before his run because it's company regulation. He can't arrive late; the perilous demerits mathematics stabs him in the soft gut. If only he could find a place to sit and read his book. It glows at the bottom of his bag, waiting for him to run his fingers through its pages. What are the beetles doing in those Egyptologists' bags? What about the one in the trouser leg? Will the second Egyptologist who wandered away manage to free himself from the sarcophagus?

The book's cloth cover lies smooth under his fingers.

He signs out at the office in the station, and the sign-out man tells him his train and his car, then hands him his slip. The fellow has an upper lateral incisor that's turned dark grey. That tooth needs extracting.

He has car Renfrew, Line no. 2501, Train no. 2, leaving at 11:00 p.m. Some high muckety-muck named this car Renfrew after some other high muckety-muck. *Car should be ready for reception of passengers at 10.00 p.m.* An eight, two, and one sleeper. Eight sections, two compartments, one drawing room, one men's washroom, one ladies' washroom. Twenty-three beds total. Montreal to Vancouver. Fastest train across the continent.

Baxter rolls the passenger list in his hand, the paper tube spilling names. Half a car until Winnipeg, then a full load from Winnipeg to Banff, and onward. Tips. A full car for most of the trip. So many berths.

Stray hairs provoke the tender skin on his ears. He should have gotten a haircut. A spotter could report him for his hair being unruly.

At 7:30 p.m. he swings up into the vestibule with his bag and his shoeshine kit.

He hangs up his coat, rolls up his shirtsleeves, trots back and forth through the narrow passageways, jumps outside the train to put the deflectors on the windows, puts up all the section numbers while an inspector double-checks the lighting in the smoker. He counts the great hidden wall of linen in its locker and marks down the count, folds towels into triangles and stacks them in the washrooms next to the washstands, sets out paper towels, cakes of toilet soap, matches, replaces emptying toilet paper rolls, wooden coat hangers. Then he makes down all the berths except for the ones in Sections 1 and 2 because those Section 1 folks won't embark until Sudbury, Lower 2 in Fort William, and Upper 4 in Winnipeg. He sweeps mattresses from the upper berths to the lower berths, folds and tucks sheets and blankets, such crisp, neat V folds, the way Edwin Drew showed him he had to. Two berths and a sofa in the Drawing Room, the berths in the compartments, the muscles in his shoulders starting to fray around Section 6, and he bangs his knuckle but good at Section 7, the small of his back whispering a tiny sliver, then he recounts the linen and towels in the linen closet.

He unfurls linen. He re-triangles hand towels, he tucks sheets. His knuckle throbs.

As Baxter labours through the sleeping car, his forehead and armpits misting with perspiration, he finds wedged in tight among the berths a tattered shirt collar, a penny, a hairpin, spilled tobacco, and crushed cigarette papers from someone who must have been trying to roll cigarettes in the dark.

An old copy of *The Messenger: World's Greatest Negro Monthly*. The magazine sears his hands. He could be fired for just being in the same room as this rag. The last porter was a dangerous *fool*. Eugene Grady splashed this magazine around and got fired from his last job in Chicago. Baxter rolls up the magazine, stuffs it into the front of his trousers, and jumps off the train. Jams it to the bottom of a garbage can and heaps the rest of the trash on top. He jumps back into his car.

The Drawing Room window ajar, his hands full with manoeuvring pillows into pillow slips, he overhears the conductor, Seamus 'Mad Mary' Magruder, talking with the engineer Stanley, and Templeton, Mad Mary's favourite porter, whose shit was jewelled treasure, Tomming as usual, with his square bulldog jaws ready to bite off a head.

– Mina was so sore, says Mad Mary, flicking ash off his cigarette. – I figured she was done with me for good.

– Mina who? asks Stanley.

– Mina, says Mad Mary, exhaling smoke. – My girl.

– Why was she sore?

– Oh Mina, says Templeton. – Why did I think her name was Enid?

Baxter can't believe the ease with which Templeton talks to Mad Mary, like Mad Mary isn't a white man. Like Templeton isn't a lowly porter. But Templeton always laughs at Mad Mary's jokes. That has to be it.

– I spilled beer on her dress.

– Enid was last year, says Stanley, spitting into the dust. – Mina sounds like Enid.

– She said I was singing too hard, says Mad Mary. – She says I'm too boisterous and I need to calm down. Says I remind her of a flea, jumping around.

Mad Mary laughs.

– Haw haw haw, laughs Templeton, slapping his stomach.

– Your girlfriends always have that *ee* sound in their names, I notice, says Stanley.

– One good way, says Templeton, – probably the best way, to make a lady angry is to spill something on her dress, says Templeton. – Hope you promised to buy her a new one. Hope you promised to marry her!

The three men wheeze with laughter.

– It was a party! says Mad Mary. – How was I supposed to know the empty bottle, the bottle *I* emptied, still had beer in it? Sometimes she's crazy as a cuckoo.

– She's the one who needs the calming down, sounds like, says Templeton.

The men's laughter dwindles away as they scuff their toes in the dirt and Mad Mary smokes his cigarettes. Stanley spits tobacco into the dust, and the men hunch their shoulders. The window letting in dust, soot, and their women problems until he slams it closed. Mad Mary beetles his woolly eyebrows at Baxter, points at his pocket watch then back at Baxter, mouthing, *Get back to work*, and Templeton's dog jowls abruptly stop their laughing.

Eugene, fresh from his no doubt delightful and filling meal at the chicken house, stalks past them, jerking up his long, thin hand to tip his straw hat like a ringmaster at a circus, and says something ridiculous about a camel, or perhaps a camera, and Stanley spits out his last bit of tobacco as he laughs, while Mad Mary only grimaces. Templeton smiles but doesn't show his teeth, so probably he's not at all pleased to see Eugene, just pretending, always pretending. Baxter yanks down the blind. He just remembered that Eugene in his fancy straw hat had called him *Martian* the last time they worked together, like being from Mars was somehow a bad thing.

Baxter stuffs his last packed sausage bun into his mouth in two bites.

Baxter will not run out of linen on this run; he's counted and double-counted, counted backwards then forwards again. He also can't order too many towels or he might get demerits. The company put Smithee in the street for ordering too many towels. They set him up! They double-crossed him! Smithee's probably only found work on fruit trains in Ontario. Or BC. Hauling peaches and pears.

8:45 p.m. Mad Mary hands him his call card, and Baxter scans it for times. Tucks it in his pocket next to his little blue instruction book. *It will be the duty of porters before departure to count clean linen,* says the little book, the little tyrant. *If figures do not agree with Linen Room count, the matter should be at once reported to Terminal Inspector who will satisfy himself that the porter's claim is correct.* He should count the linen again. There's no time.

9:00 p.m. Baxter sets out his step box, uniform smart, all the gold buttons securely sewn and gleaming.

9:00 p.m. One car up, Templeton sets out his step box, uniform smart, all the gold buttons securely sewn and gleaming, his dog mouth firmly set. Mad Mary Magruder's Uncle Tom spy. Baxter nods hello, and Templeton clenches his jaws into pretend-friendly. Templeton never gets demerits, the toady. Baxter could never gulp down as many toads as that.

9:00 p.m. A porter Baxter's never met sets out his step box the car behind Baxter's. The porter's face and hands studded and scattered with freckles upon freckles with an extra helping of freckles. The porter waves a hearty hello at Baxter, scattering his freckles in a shower around him. Baxter's seeing things already.

9:00 p.m. Two cars behind, Eugene Grady sets out his step box with a flourish. He hates this job so much, his hatred steams from his body like vapour from a tin roof after rain. Baxter should avoid him. Baxter should try to talk to him. Repair the tear in their friendship.

A neat appearance is essential. Shoes shined, uniform pressed, cap set rightly on the head and an upright posture create a good impression.

9:01 p.m. Another porter Baxter knows, Ferdinand, is a speck in the distance, too many cars away. Ferdinand sets out his step box. Ferdinand is a strange, appealing man who flies a kite on stopovers, even on Sundays instead of going to church.

Baxter tips his hat to Eugene, but irritation moults off Eugene in great slices, his disdain ghosting his face as he greets the passengers, carries their suitcases, and hefts up other bits and bobs into the car.

A passenger puffs his cheeks out in frustration as he accidentally tips his bag and scatters papers, clothes, and coins that roll all over the platform. Mad Mary raises an arm to hail a Red Cap to corral the mess and leaves Baxter to offer his elbow to passengers and catch at their grasping hands as they climb up his step box, let him feed them into the car's maw.

All aboard.

Between 9:00 and 10:55 p.m., Mad Mary inspects more tickets on the platform. Baxter can't help thinking about *The Scarab from Jupiter*. The book says there's a scarab constellation with Jupiter right in the middle of it, but he's never seen it. He's stashed the scarab-stamped book at the bottom of his bag. His thoughts twist and turn a little screwy as he greets passenger after passenger and funnels them into the dark shell of the train. Which passenger might have a head full of Robot cogs instead of brain, or which passenger might be a Jupiterian scarab beetle disguised as a honeymooner, ready to kill him and eat him in one bite. The waves and ripples of passengers' smells and heat as they swish by him, his trying to sense before it's too late which ones might yell at him for fetching a cup of water the wrong way, which one will be an undercover spotter out to get him fired for an eyebrow hair out of place or a spider-webbed sconce. Ten demerits and $101 to go.

Mad Mary's pasty whey temples trickle with sweat as he directs passengers to and fro on the platform and sorts out tickets, the brass label on his cap glittering in the station lamplight, the hiss of the train's engine up ahead. Red Caps fuss as they load and unload the passengers' bags and trunks, stalling for perhaps a dime, a trio of nickels. A few infuriating brown pennies. Another Red Cap, so young he still has womb slime under his collar, stands alone to the side, moving so extraordinarily slowly he must be new, maybe he's sick. Like a fish that won't swim away as you approach it closer and closer and then grab it. Is that Red Cap even real? No. He has gills on both sides of his throat. Baxter turns to the next passengers clogging up the queue, and the Red Cap melts into a truss, which of course is what he was all along.

A pair of women, mother and daughter, both with hair the colour of cigars, the daughter's coiled under a feathered hat, the mother's surprisingly short for an older woman, choke up the queue to car Renfrew as the daughter bickers with her mother while standing on Baxter's step box, then stepping off, then on, up then down again, Baxter certain she'll topple any moment in her feathery hat, while her mother stamps her foot in irritation at her and the daughter tosses her hands up in the air in a tantrum, her mouth in a sneer, a line of passengers clotting behind them in a long, whipping tail. A hatbox says *Tupper*.

– Good evening, Mrs. and Miss Tupper, says Baxter. – Ladies.

The Tuppers cut off their quarrel mid-sentence as they spin away from each other to fix instead on him. Then they launch up and into the vestibule in a flurry of whispered ladylike cussing, and Baxter checks the ticket belonging to the next person in line.

A man with a long white beard who looks like Saint Nicholas.

A man named *Bland*: the tag on his Boston bag trumpeting his name. Mr. Bland, barely able to lift his head from his important papers.

Newlyweds, their faces pink and round. He can tell they are newly wed because the man announces their newlyweddedness: This is my *wife*, Mrs. Lewington, he says.

– And this is my *husband*, Mr. Lewington, she says, crinkling her eyes at him.

– After you, *Mrs*. Lewington, my *wife*, says the husband.

– Thank you, my *husband*, Mr. Lewington.

The husband bows to her, gleeful, and tucks one of her hands in the crook of his elbow.

The last passengers aboard, Baxter clears his throat, ascends the vestibule steps, and directs passengers to their razor-folded beds like a policeman in traffic choreographing motor vehicles, bicycles, humans, and horses. Baxter politely instructs the weary-looking Mr. Bland that he did not book the Drawing Room, he is in Section

4 with the other pauperish well-to-do who paid only for Sections, not the Drawing Room, nor the middling-well-to-do two compartments. Bland man's face flushes blood-sausage purple, as though he could argue his way into the more expensive room, but then he straggles toward the opposite end of the car, ducking into corners and bends in the passageway, flattening and walking sideways like a crab as other passengers also flatten and crab-walk past him. He is a poor well-to-do person. The poorest of the well-to-do people who ride this train. His Boston bag alone is probably worth months and months of Baxter's wages and tips. Probably two hundred dollars. Poor, poor man.

In Section 3, the young husband Mr. Lewington makes his young wife Mrs. Lewington climb the ladder into the upper berth while he settles himself into the lower berth, *My back!* he says. Mrs. Lewington clutches her way up the upholstered ladder into the plush, windowless coffin suspended on chains directly above her new husband. Unchivalrous bastard should have taken the upper.

Mad Mary Magruder calls, *All aboard*, the *oooar* drawn out until it sounds almost mournful. Baxter tucks away the step box and heaves the trap, then the door, closed. The train judders, then sighs. Baxter stands alone in the steel burgundy bubble of the vestibule, swaying with the train as it rumbles out of the station. He inhales a deep breath.

He kicks the metal wall. Hard.

He bends down to polish the toe of his shoe with his thumb. Flourishes a green duster out of his pocket to polish the scuff off the painted, riveted wall. Eighty-eight hours and forty-five minutes to go. The floor darkens and drops away, then rises up, gurgling with light. He can feel vomit rising up into his throat, but he covers his mouth, closes his eyes until his nausea passes, until the waves of sleepiness hitting him recede with the tide. The floor settles flat, settles solid and hard beneath his feet.

He yanks at the bottom button of his coat.

He straightens his jacket, resets his cap on his head, then strides into the passageway. He changes from his blue uniform coat into the white summer uniform coat. He saunters past the ladies' washroom and into the tube of shelf after shelf of passengers, while the train speeds and sparks over the rails in the dark.

The passengers continue to bustle themselves into the rows of smooth beds he's prepared that bloom from the ceiling and every wall, the aisle of drapes shrouding the beds in the sections. They settle into their soft, mattressed shelves with their suitcases and boxes, their hats, their nightshirts and dressing gowns, their unsolicited opinions, and their bottomless pits of well-to-do and phony-well-to-do needs:

– Porter, you must wake me at the correct time, the porter on the train from Chicago forgot, remember, Willy? That porter wasn't right in the head if you ask me.

– Porter, fetch me a new pillow. This one's sticking me with feathers.

– Oh porter, are we going to be on time? What time will we get to Moosomin?

– George, how far away to the club car? I need a drink.

Click, thinks Baxter. He is a clicking Robot, created to serve. He is a whirring automaton, screwed together to entertain.

He runs last-minute errands as they settle into sleep. He shifts the ladder up and down the aisle as passengers ascend and descend for water, for the washroom, two passengers snoring already.

The passengers' unshined shoes and boots wash up along the shores of the curtains, drop into place behind the small metal doors along the passageway of compartments and the Drawing Room. The passengers whisper and slide into sleep, rustling, snoring, and sleeptalking in their neat, curtained rows or behind their deluxe mahogany doors.

In eighty-eight hours and five minutes he will land on the other side of the country. This run west as long as a Portuguese man-of-war tentacle, long and painful.

He blends into the flocked wallpaper, just another shadow ambling down the hallway of drawn berth curtains, and he gathers two pairs of boots or shoes at a time, just like it says in the instruction book, even though it's inefficient as the devil. He scrawls the section numbers with soap on the soles. In the smoker he settles himself in the green leather chair and shines shoes. He isn't *obliged* to shine shoes, but the company *expects* him to shine shoes. Shining shoes means tips, and no complaints, and keeping his job. Not shining shoes means becoming that fired porter James. A free, free man with severely diminished prospects. Working as a chimney sweep in Calgary, last Baxter heard.

He burrows into the still-warm shoes, brushing, rubbing, the repetition of boot after shoe after boot a sick, slick rhythm.

The bell rings. He springs up, wiping bootblack off his hands. One of the little metal arrows on his call board points toward the Drawing Room.

The lady in the Drawing Room can't sleep because of the temperature, and she wants another blanket.

– Why's it so cold? she asks.

It ain't, he wants to say. It's August, for the love of Mike! He's pickling in the heat in the closeness of the train.

– I tried to turn up the heat, but it's not functioning, she says, pulling her wrap closer around her shoulders.

– I'll try my best, he says.

He sidles into the Drawing Room, and the chill hits him. Now that he's standing in the room, standing still and not busy stuffing pillows into pillow slips or counting out sets of sheets, it's true that the room seems to purr with cold. It reminds him of his parents' house growing up, and how he always needed to escape to the laughing heat of Aunt Arimenta's house. She never liked his parents' house, and told his mother so. Aunt Arimenta said it was cold-hearted. This Drawing Room is cold-hearted. Fiddling with a thermostat won't fix this room, drafty in the middle of a roasting summer night.

He kneels and, blocking her and her husband's view with his shoulders, he taps and bangs his keys against the steam pipe.

– That should do the trick, madam, he says.

He unfolds the list in his pocket. She'll be on this train all the way to Vancouver, the very end. He's stuck with her like a raspberry seed caught in a molar.

He nicknames her Judy, like Punch and Judy, because she and her husband are so shiny, her shiny red cheeks and her husband's red nose shining in the dark behind her. The way their lips stay fixed even when they ask him for the third time when they'll make it to Sicamous, British Columbia. Punch's sister lives in Sicamous and she'll be waiting on the platform for a quick hello. Baxter himself hasn't seen any of his own cousins for almost ten years, just a birthday letter here and there on both sides. Punch growls out a snore before Baxter's even closed the room door, the cold no problem for him, clearly. Baxter scoops up their shoes from the locker beside their door.

He dabs shoeshine paste on Punch's shoes: creamy brown uppers with stitching that looks like fairy fingers sewed them, but the soles thinned almost to holes, the heels worn down at the outer edges. Sometimes the wear on some soles surprises him, the shoes of these opulent people hinting at their secrets. He swipes the shoeshine rag at his own feet, his toes glittering in the gloom.

He delivers the pairs of shoes as he completes them, slides them back under curtained berths, opens the individual lockers and shoves them in, toes to the front, heels to the back.

He blacks boots, polishes, he buffs, he polishes again.

Edwin Drew once told him and a group of other student porters a story about how one time he collected all the shoes from a car full of passengers, and then when he went to return the shoes, saw that the passengers' car had uncoupled from the rest of the train when the train stopped at the last station, and that he now had a bag full of shoes and no passengers, and the passengers had no shoes.

Baxter and the other greenhorns shuddered with laughter, Edwin Drew grabbing Baxter by the arm to hold himself up as he guffawed, and Baxter feels buttery inside at the memory, at the glowing warmth and strength of Edwin Drew's grip through his sleeve.

As he returns the pairs of shoes one by one, the fact that he doesn't have enough brown shoeshine to last out this run picks at the back of his head. Eugene two cars over might have extra brown shine. Yes, he can ask Eugene for some brown shoeshine. He will brush aside Eugene's childishness, his sulkiness. After all, as porters they are all brothers, Eugene chattering on about *the Brotherhood*.

Once upon a time Eugene still treated Baxter like one of his own: he taught Baxter new card games whenever they met up at porters' quarters, then he'd lick him at the exact same card games. He joked with Baxter like a little brother about the books Baxter read, how his nose was always in a book or a magazine and he seemed to like books better than people.

– Maybe if you weren't reading so many weird books you'd find yourself a wife, Martian! Eugene would say. – Har har! Pass me that deck of cards. I have another game I can teach you to lose.

Eugene fanning the cards out on the table between them, his straw sailor hat perched toward the back of his head, his bony fingers and wrists flicking and dancing in the air as the cards fell in precise, geometric formation.

– Nothing wrong with being from Mars, Baxter would say, and Eugene would just snicker, – Sure, Martian.

Then, after the Edwin Drew matter happened, Eugene started making a face like Baxter was a charred piece of meat whenever he saw Baxter. Suddenly. Sadly. Baxter never knew who told Eugene; it could have been Eugene's sister, Edwin's wife. Or Edwin himself.

Edwin would never do that.

Baxter passes through the vestibules between their cars and almost trips over a pair of men's shoes sprawled in his way, the shoes polished so hard the uppers mirror his face. Before he touches them, his face and fingers reflected back oblong and jagged in the leather, he realizes the soles glow like embers, they don't belong to anybody on this train, and so he steps over them so they won't contaminate him. No one else will bother with or even notice figmental shoes like these.

He worries that one day the lack of sleep will drive him into the lunatic asylum.

At first Eugene pretends not to hear Baxter as he buffs and turns a shoe, his elbows pointed out too far, then drops it next to its mate, his feet buried in multiple pairs of passengers' shoes, exactly the way porters are *not* supposed to do it.

– Got none to spare, says Eugene. His mouth flattens into a disappointed slice. Baxter's chest contracts. Eugene has the longest eyelashes Baxter has ever seen on a man.

Eugene's call board chimes, and he tosses the shoe back into the pile. He unfolds his stick-figure self up from the stool, one limb at a time, not hurrying one bit. Baxter retreats from the doorway as Eugene pushes past him.

Baxter returns to his car, the ground rocking as he moves. He'll ask the freckled porter to watch his car.

– Boo! says the freckled porter, leering out of the dark.

Freckles even sprinkle his eyelids.

– D'you have any brown shoeshine I could use? asks Baxter. – What's your name?

– Freckles, says Freckles. – No. Watch my car. I need to go down.

– All right.

Freckles snaps his fingers. Retreats into the dark, his freckles splashing out a trail behind him.

Baxter sits on a hard stool at the end of the aisle in the Renfrew, monitoring the walls of curtains for any hijinks, waiting for the infernal bell for his car *and* for Freckles's. His head bobbing with sleep.

Five seconds.

The call-board bell rings. The tiny metal arrow sits tilted next to Section 6. Baxter hurries to Section 6.

Upper 6 needs the ladder.

On his way back to his stool, he catches up his book from the locker. Cracks it open. A golden scarab has just crawled up into the nostril of the Egyptologist trapped in the sarcophagus!

Baxter has travelled this run once before. He'll come close to truly cracking in half somewhere between Regina and Moose Jaw, the gagging and uneasy stomach from lack of proper food and sleep. He blinks. Savours the tiny nap behind that blink, his eyelids scratching. His head nods.

The WC door slams.

His head bobs up. A man, tailed by a woman, slink by in the passageway, humming out of tune, the woman in a dressing gown, the man fully clothed in a suit, the woman's hands holding the man's hips.

He doesn't see them.

These are among the many things he does not see when he rides the stool: married men slipping into the berths or compartments of women not their wives. Passengers wealthier than Croesus pilfering towels and silver CPR spoons like the youngest bastard sons of a family of chicken pluckers.

Baxter doesn't see sweat and semen stains on train linen, human manure, blood, or spills of urine. He doesn't speak of liquor heads or decrepitude or ineptitude or plain old mediocrity dressed up as something else as he mops it up, scrapes it, soaps it down, throws it out.

He's picked up undergarments. A passenger's forgotten garters, sanitary belts, stretched-out perfumed stockings once shocked him, but now so many women ride the sleepers that he touches these things without seeing them, cares only that the train is moving on time, that he can collect some money crumbs and get off this train.

He doesn't hear the whispered story of a rare trainman, rare as a jellyfish with teeth, slipping, invited, into a lady's compartment. During the darkest edge of a blue hunter's moon night when another porter once asked Baxter to watch his car while he got up to hijinks because a lady invited him in, and that porter was pals with the conductor, who resolved to look the other way. Baxter's stomach convulses for anyone caught with these lethal, bejewelled white women. He's heard sometimes these white women work as undercover spotters.

The rolling of the train makes women romantic, Edwin Drew once told him.

And, Baxter, startled, violently thought of men suspended by their necks or by their heels from trees, white men's knees kneeling into and snapping their necks. Men dragged until they're shredded past death.

The bell rings. He crosses the vestibule to Freckles's car to fetch a mixture of Bromo-Seltzer for a freckled, ginger-haired man. Ginger-hair freckles, not dark-skin freckles like Freckles's. Baxter shifts and slides among the folds of the curtains, the shadows, just like a scarab from Jupiter with overdeveloped, overly sharp mandibles. Yes.

When he's sat back down on his stool, he turns pages in his book, but no matter how much he flips back and forth through the pages, he can't find the beetle crawling into the man's sinus. He placed the bookmark in the crease of the very last page for some reason.

When he works on a train, Baxter doesn't see the particular curve of a male passenger's buttocks, another porter's achingly tempting Adam's apple, shoulders straining too-tight shirtsleeves. He does not look at crotches, no matter how tight the trousers, he does not hear the occasional panting of a man alone in the WC with only the hopper for company.

That one time last spring Baxter didn't see a ten-dollar bill as a compartment passenger – some kind of parliamentarian from Ottawa – casually extracted the bill from a bill case and slid it over to Baxter along the edge of a commode. Or what Baxter didn't see in order to earn that bill.

But he always has shiny new dimes in his pocket, and he's well on his way to saving enough for dentistry school. He pokes his eyeglasses back up his nose. Flips through more pages. He can't wait for a proper job instead of this job, which was supposed to be only a summer job. Aunt Arimenta wouldn't be too happy knowing that his summer job, the one he took so that he could pay for university, became his twenty-four-hour, fall, winter, and spring job too. She would clamp down so hard on her pipe the stem would snap in two if she knew he was scrubbing out lavatories for a living, even if he did get to travel while doing it. He was able to enrol in two years of university, but then he followed the advice of Edwin Drew for a while, and stayed in the job to collect the instant money. He wanted to *be* Edwin Drew.

But now he's back on track. Maybe he'll work with prosthetic teeth! Maybe he'll make two hundred dollars a month with a new prosthetic teeth invention! He'll never have to clean a hopper again, never get called *George* ever ever again.

The train rumbles over the tracks, shoots through the darkness. Sometimes moving so quickly they manage to break the time barrier, shooting backward in time, and that's why the run takes so long.

He flips through the pages of his book until he finds his place again. While the Egyptologist asphyxiating in the sarcophagus has a gold scarab eating through the whorls of his chemical brain, the Queen Scarab has climbed to the top of an Egyptian pyramid to lay Her eggs. Baxter's skin prickles when the Scarab emits a flash of light from Her mandibles and incinerates an archaeologist named Cecil.

But he closes his eyelids. He can't help it.

A flash of Baxter curled up on the sofa in the smoker and the shriek of the bell splitting his head like a train wheel squealing on a steel track the second his cheek touches the leather upholstery. Because if Mad Mary Magruder catches him sleeping, Baxter will end up a chimney sweep like that porter James. Or plucking chickens. Everywhere but dentistry school.

He fingers his watch.

He crosses the vestibule between his and Freckles's cars, from the Renfrew to the Redfern, to wake up Freckles.

– My turn, says Baxter.

– Awww, says Freckles, pulling his mandible down in an impossibly big yawn. – Yeah, yeah. Don't let the bed bite. Don't let the bed bite the bugs.

Baxter bangs back to his own lavatory, collapses sideways onto the seat reeking of tobacco smoke and bottoms, no mattress, no blanket, no sheets.

His eyes slam shut.

He dreams he's reading a book; he's split open his book to where he's parked his bookmark, but the bookmark is a long tongue, and the words squiggle down the pages because the book is crying.

Freckles shakes him awake, and he wants to squiggle with tears too.

Five minutes between bells for the ladder.

Kuzyk the waiter pokes his head into the room. – Breakfast, Kuzyk sniffs, and propels himself away.

6:25 a.m. Baxter will go for breakfast but buy dinner somewhere at one of the station lunch counters along the way. Can he afford bacon? If he decides he wants bacon, will it be good bacon or burned bacon? Will it even have any meat on it? His brain flips over, tugs blankets up over its face.

The train whistles as it approaches a crossing. A passenger abruptly bleats in her sleep.

Baxter stands up from his stool: one night almost down, three more nights to go.

The train hoots as it rumbles into the morning.

– Watch my car, he tells Freckles.

Freckles kicks at him for a joke, then shoos him away.

The porters eat their breakfast or drink coffee behind a curtain in the dining car. Eugene and Templeton. Another porter he doesn't know: – Name's A.P., says A.P. He has a voice so raspy it seems unnatural, like his vocal cords should hurt, rubbing against each other, sounds like.

Templeton and A.P. chortle and murmur over some shared joke that makes Templeton laugh silently, but so hard tears seep from his eyes. Eugene holds his coffee cup in front of his mouth, nothing but his eyelashed eyes showing above the china cup.

– Martian, says Eugene, nodding his head in Baxter's direction.

– Welcome, says Templeton, baring his teeth.

Baxter swallows pieces of dry roll, slurps up the spoonful of scorched beans, scoops his peeled, boiled egg into his mouth whole. His stomach bubbles queerly. The plates never hold enough food, only half portions. He can't afford the bacon.

Eugene reminds them all that he, Eugene, has a degree from Howard University. – And don't you forget it. A degree in *law*.

He twirls his napkin in the air. Once.

Templeton belches a laugh, but the laugh is empty, the man is always laughing, especially when there's nothing to laugh at. His jowls flap as he bites into his last shred of toast.

Templeton has a degree in mathematics. His original plan was to do the accounting for some company. Baxter wants to stop up his ears with candlesticks or golden beetles just to drown out the swaggering. Baxter doesn't tell any of them that he attended university for two years and then left. Apparently to clean toilets on trains for white people. He sighs. A.P. chases a last bean on his plate.

– You've got shoeshine under your nails, Martian, says Eugene, spreading his own fingers out, his nails scrubbed clean.

There, a line of shoeshine under Baxter's thumbnail. Baxter scrapes it quickly with a toothpick, embarrassed.

– Passengers aren't supposed to see traces of the actual *labour*, Eugene says, drawing a long hair out of his oatmeal and draping it in the middle of the table.

– Shut your mouth, Eugene, says Templeton, ever smiling. He gulps from his cup of coffee.

– Nice talking with you all! A.P. rasps, and dashes away for his life, his bowl of oatmeal still half full.

– Why should the working man be paid for his *labour*, Eugene sneers.

– I said, says Templeton, baring his teeth as he jabs between them with a toothpick, – knock it off with the Brotherhood hogwash.

Baxter stops scraping his fork against his plate for the last smears of sauce. The handle of his fork clinking against his cup.

– Now that's the stuff of weird tales, huh, Martian, says Eugene, jabbing Baxter with his pointy elbow. – Someone should write a story about a man getting paid properly for his labour.

Templeton raises the corner of his lip. He jabs an index finger in Eugene's direction. – I'm watching you, he says.

– Need to pry your eyeballs out of your rectum first, says Eugene.

– You better make sure you mind your Ps and Qs. Wouldn't want you out of work again, what with your wives at both ends of the line, Eugene Grady.

Eugene curls a fist.

– Don't even consider it, laughs Templeton, swiping his mouth with a napkin. – I will beat you into mincemeat. You watch out for this one, Templeton says to Baxter, flicking his thumb at Eugene.

Baxter bows his head and scrapes with a fresh toothpick under the nail of his index finger.

Templeton pushes away, stalks into the depths of the train.

– Thinks he's the snake's hips, says Eugene. – Nincompoop.

Sipping the last dregs, he contemplates Baxter over the rim of his cup. The silence bumpy and awkward in spite of the regular chatter of the train.

Baxter wants to ask him if he's seen Edwin Drew lately. How is Edwin Drew doing. Has Edwin Drew asked about him.

– You just think you can sit by and let the rest of us do the hard work, don't you, Baxter? says Eugene.

Baxter circles his spoon in his grey coffee.

Eugene wipes his mouth and pushes away from the table. – He was never your friend, you know, says Eugene. – He boohooed to my sister first chance he got.

– Who?

– You *know* who, says Eugene, and he pushes his way past the curtain that hides the porters from the passengers, the curtain flapping large, as though Eugene had punched it on his way out.

Baxter sits alone at the table, the perpetual rumble and rocking of the car around him. A sad carapace hardens around him, his heart already encased in a thick rind. Eugene and his wives and worker labour talk and Edwin Drew the blank spot in the middle.

Baxter pushes away from the table to standing. He stamps his feet, first the right, then the left. Just like a Robot.

DAY TWO

(SUDBURY TO WINNIPEG)

The sun cracks open. Baxter scratches away a plum tree sprouting behind his ear.

An orchard, the trees weighted with phosphorescent red fruit, speeds past outside the window. The freakish trees tick by, row by row.

The train is still chugging miles outside of Sudbury when passengers start rousing and spilling from their berths. This run not even a day old, and three towels have already been thieved, and Baxter tries not to swear out loud when he mule-kicks the vestibule wall, three times, one for each towel. Replacing towels alone will eat up his tips!

He dashes up and down the aisle with the ladder as passengers slide down and out of their berths, breaking through the draperies, carrying toothbrushes, razors, face cream, dressing cases. The skin around their eyes harnessed in that bloated morning look.

Passengers board in Sudbury at 7:00 a.m., and he settles them into Section 2.

Water rushes into basins, into deluxe three-minute shower baths. Dropped razor blades, bars of soap. He shields his eyes from unlucky flashes of women's knees and nipples, their naked armholes, as they sail about the ladies' lavatory in front and around him the way one sails in front and around a piece of furniture.

He *isn't* more than a piece of furniture. He is the same as a commode.

The passengers stagger around, amateurs on their shaky legs as they manoeuvre the narrow passageway, the train's constant shimmying and joggling. Passengers from other cars, white passengers, one coloured passenger, cut through his car on their way to other glamorous, scenic, well-fed and well-watered parts of the train.

– First call for breakfast, calls Kuzyk as he sweeps down the aisle. – First call for breakfast. First call for breakfast.

Kuzyk sways with the movement of the train as he strides, as the morning blusters into day.

Baxter wipes down the long washstand in the men's with a cloth and scrubs at a queer, drying splatter with a sprinkle of Old Dutch, then dries off and polishes the basins, just like Edwin Drew taught him during training at Union Station on that out-of-service sleeper pulled over and away on a siding.

– Second call for breakfast! Kuzyk sings out.

Then later, – Third call for breakfast!

Baxter hustles and sweats, making up berths while the passengers gorge on their breakfasts of fried kidney, piles of eggs, hollandaise and Madeira sauces, his shoulder muscles throbbing. Trees and bushes green like tight lettuce heads, like broccoli heads, rush past the train on both sides while he stuffs a pillow into a clean pillow slip.

The trees don't care.

He flattens himself as the passenger Judy and her shiny puppet cheeks move to pass him. – Come ahead, madam, he says, – come ahead.

The hot air of the day has already begun. He'll have to turn on the fans.

But Judy doesn't pass him, she stops right beside him. So close he can smell her blueberry-and-maple-syrup breath.

– Porter, she says.

– Yes, madam?

– I'm in the Drawing Room. The temperature in our room still has not improved since I brought it to your attention last night.

– I'm so sorry, madam, he says, slapping a hand against his breast in what he hopes looks like contrition. – I increased the heat immediately after you informed me.

– I would like to speak with the conductor. I believe you have been lying to me about turning on the heat.

Fear squeezes his stomach. Her droplet earrings shake and tinkle with fury.

– Yes, madam.

Too much sweat slides down his back, his shirt sticking to him, as she marches away, her jewelled hands clenched into determined fists, the earrings sparking as she shunts her stuffed puppet body through sunbeam after sunbeam trumpeting through the windows. He clutches his belly. His stomach *hurts*.

While Mad Mary tranquilizes Judy with his best conductor butter-and-Béarnaise voice, Baxter tries not to think about the reason she'll have him dismissed, the infinite possibilities listed in the instruction manual in his pocket that could earn him those last ten demerits or his job completely lost, page 17, *disloyalty, dishonesty, immorality, insubordination, incompetence, gross carelessness, untruthfulness.*

A man whose face Baxter doesn't even see in his blur of panic tells him that the toilet needs some attending, – If you know what I mean, adds the man out the side of his mouth.

Baxter wrinkles his nose as he wipes the hopper seat with a paper towel and dumps the paper towel down the hole, cleans up newspapers around the toilet bowl, folds them, and stuffs them under his arm. A newspaper, a *Canadian Homes and Gardens* magazine, a *Manchester Guardian.* The WC isn't a library!

She could get him for *dishonesty* and *untruthfulness.* If she is theatrical, perhaps *gross carelessness.*

He scrubs behind the toilet with more paper towels. His thumb nicks on an edge of folded card, wedged between the wall and the baseboard next to the toilet.

A postcard. Folded in half. He extracts it, his hands still damp from cleaning the toilet, the inside of his nose still puckered from revulsion.

He unfolds the postcard. His thumb grips it.

Two naked men, one Negro, one white, entwined among bedsheets, their mouths soldered to one another's cocks.

His penis lunges into a panicked half salute.

He quickly stuffs the photo down the back of his pants.

He should throw the thing down the toilet with the slops.

He'll discard it at the next stop. Fort William. He'll report it to Mad Mary.

He finishes his cleaning, his hands trembling, his chest tight. The toilet seat shines. Just like Edwin Drew taught him.

He moves the postcard from the back of his pants to the inside pocket of his jacket. Just touching the image splashes him. He clatters his broom, steps out of the doorway as a passenger slams the closet door closed behind him.

He continues sweeping with his trembling fingers, continues wiping, his brain unhooked from its proper place. The postcard scorches the inside of his coat's inside pocket. It glows fiercely, scalding his chest.

His bell rings, the little metal arrow for the Drawing Room turned askew on his board. Judy. And Punch.

– Porter, says Judy. – I am *freezing*.

She's wrapped herself in two blankets, and she wants another one, and she wants the heat turned up.

– Porter, she says, – the cold in here is outrageous. Listen to my teeth chatter. See the goosebumps on my arm.

Baxter gently sways in the doorway with the rattling of the car, the air exhaling from her compartment. – Perhaps you might consider visiting the solarium, madam, he says. – Where there's plenty of sun. It is quite lovely indeed, madam, and one of the finest features of this train.

She reaches a bare forearm toward him, gold and silver bangles tinkling on her wrist. He flinches. He can't believe he just flinched. He hopes she hasn't noticed. He hopes she won't complain about that too.

– Oh, I've alarmed you, she says, a gold watch on a chain around her neck bouncing against her bosom. – Don't mind my temper tantrum from earlier. You don't have to worry about me. I come from a long line of abolitionists. I both love and pray every day for my brothers and sisters of the Negro race.

She smiles at him in a glossy, grandmotherly way that claws his lungs.

She leans in so close he can see his reflection in the varnish on her forehead, he can feel the hot vapour of her breath collect on his cheek.

– I have read an entire issue of *The Messenger* from cover to cover, she whispers. – I have also read half an issue of *The Crisis*, but then I have to admit the writing became a little too florid. Mr. Randolph has done *marvellous* things. As has *Mr. Robinson* and his friends. And the *Order of Sleeping Car Porters*. You see? I know all about your people.

Her left eyelid drops in an uncanny, exaggerated wink. She makes him want to shed his own skin, quickly, so he can dash away from her giant pink puppet-self.

– I'll increase the temperature again, madam, he says. He pretends to scratch his temple, but really he delicately wipes away a sweat droplet.

In his seat next to the window flashing broccoli trees and parsley bushes, Punch ignores Baxter and loudly rumples his newspaper as he turns a page.

– Judith, harrumphs Punch (*Judith!* thinks Baxter), – the temperature in here is *normal*.

– Then why are you wearing a pullover? Judy retorts.

Who was the male passenger who asked Baxter to clean the hopper, *If you know what I mean?* Perhaps Punch slid the postcard in behind the baseboard. Perhaps Punch has a coat pocket stuffed with other postcards. Perhaps the train will be raided by the police, and they'll rip open suitcase after suitcase packed with cards, all those naked men fluttering and gliding away in the wind. Perhaps he could see another one of these extraordinary postcards, just as a curiosity.

Judy with her dangerous sympathies will be his downfall on this run.

The passageway virtually ripples with the August heat. The sunlight mirrored so bright it makes a noise every time he passes through a sunbeam.

But the cold, moist air from Judy's compartment taps him on the cheek, startles him. How it creeps around his ears even though the train pushes through the sunny late-summer landscape, while other passengers rip off their shawls and jackets, grumbling about the rising heat in this luxurious, travelling cage.

He hustles away from Judy and her room's coldness, pretending he's leaving to turn the lever on the heat.

In the lavatories, he replaces slimy half cakes of soap with fresh ones, wipes down the washbasins, the mirrors, refills a toilet paper roll.

He discovers the missing towels. Every single missing one of them, sopping wet and heaped on the floor in the vestibule by some passenger who must think he or she's at home, and that towels don't cost good money.

He jams all the towels into a soiled pillow slip, against the rules, but his irritation is peaking and his patience has frayed. Then he shoves them into the bottom of the linen closet, next to a man curled and shivering in a ball even though he glows like a coal on a fire. The one who owns the shiny, glowing shoes in the vestibule no doubt. Baxter closes the door. Locks it, and the figmental man, away with a crisp turn of his key.

Baxter claps his hand to his mouth to hide his yawn. His hand smells of urine. Of hot ice.

In the car Redfern, Baxter nearly bumps into Templeton carrying a bottle of fancy whisky and a glass on a silver tray. He could work for six months, seven months, eight months, eight years, and still not be able to afford that bottle of whisky. It might as well cost two hundred dollars. Baxter doesn't want to ask, he doesn't want to tangle with Templeton any more than he has to, but he can't resist.

– Who's *that* for? Baxter asks.

– Famous writer, Templeton says, his jowls aflap.

Baxter clamps his tongue between his teeth in excitement. Fat bushes whir by outside the window.

– Who? he asks.

– Jules Verne, says Templeton.

– Jules Verne is dead.

– Oh. Then I guess it's not him. Ha ha ha!

Templeton hustles away with his luxurious bottle, still chortling. Baxter wants to grab that bottle by the neck, drink it, then smash it through one of these fussy, flowery windows.

Baxter's insides shrivel as he trudges back to his car. Maybe Templeton stuffed the postcard in the baseboard to mock him, to trap him. No. *Eugene* would do this kind of thing. Eugene would love to see Baxter squirm.

There's no name for the feeling inside him because of this card, because of this job. If he could, if she were still alive, he would describe his insides to his aunt Arimenta, and she would tell him the name for when your insides feel the same as a wide orchard of blighted fruit trees. – We'll just cut out the rot, says Arimenta, peeling the spotty black skin off the top mango in a bowl of mealy mangos. – Just cut out the rot and go for the good.

His first bite of mango tastes bitter, but he chews and swallows and eats some more anyway because she's the one who's peeling and cutting it up for him, the juice dripping off his fingers and tendrilling down his forearms. Arimenta chews too, grimacing.

– Guess there's some things you just can't fix. Oh well, she says, and smacks his cheek with a big, juicy kiss.

She takes another bite, and chews some more.

– Don't tell your mother, she says, looking across the blighted trees, but I'm going to leave you money when I pass.

She spears another slice and puts it in her mouth. She suddenly laughs. – Oh, she says, – here's a good one!

And she passes him the rest of the mango.

After the first call for dinner, Baxter starts breaking down berths again as passengers take turns disappearing for their dinners.

Two naked men tangled together.

He squashes a finger between a wall and a descending panel. He smothers a yell. His eyes water.

Passengers straggle back from their gluttonous eating, fragrant with roast pork, poached fish, strawberry pie for dessert, and slither their bloated bellies into their plush shelves for the night. He could gobble up a whole suckling pig right now.

– I haven't eaten so much in ages! says Miss Tupper, swanning behind her mother toward their section, her hand on her belly, her feathery hat still parked on her head. She slides, behind-first, into her curtained berth. Her mother climbs up the ladder in her silky kimona, stands for a moment at the top surveying the train car, and then dives in, the silk slithering in after her.

Templeton asks him to watch his car while he goes down.

Baxter pauses before he says yes. Templeton the laughing toady. The conductor's favourite porter.

Baxter tips out of a cuspidor blobs of soggy, chewed-up tobacco, glutinous ashes, and cigar ends into the men's hopper until the cuspidor rings empty, the ties speeding by below, and he rinses out the remaining slobber with disinfectant he also splashes out onto the ties.

He settles onto the hopper. Rechecks the latch on the door. He slowly picks the postcard out of his pocket, unfolds it. Those bodies in the dim light. Who are these men? His own hips roll with the rocking of the train. He wipes his behind, the nighttime tracks speeding by beneath his naked backside. He shuts the WC door behind him. He checks his call board. Moves to his stool, sags sideways briefly before yanking himself up.

The bell rings, the Drawing Room.

– Are you sure you've turned up the heat? Judy asks. – This cannot continue.

Punch gurgles out a snore, a naked furry leg, a bare horned foot hanging over the side of his bed.

– I'll check it again, Baxter says. He tries not to shiver. He struggles against every artery pulsing under his skin to tell her there is no way to fix this problem, that some places are lucky and some are unlucky, and that she is unlucky in this room.

He taps the thermostat, moves the arrow around, practising hopeless legerdemain for this poor woman.

– That should work, he says.

– I'm sure it will this time! she says. She draws her shawl closer around her shoulders.

He bids her goodnight, then perches back on his stool, rubbing his hands together to warm them back up.

Right at that moment, Mad Mary pokes in his head. Grunts, disappointed he didn't catch Baxter sleeping.

– There's heating problems in the Drawing Room, says Baxter.

– Heating? Are you off your head? asks Mad Mary. – It's a frying pan in here.

– I'm just repeating what the passenger said.

– I don't like your tone.

– My apologies, Mr. Magruder.

– That's *right*, says Mad Mary. He clicks his ticket puncher in Baxter's direction, then clumps away.

Baxter flips through *The Scarab from Jupiter* so that he won't have time to think about the postcard in his breast pocket, slotted right over his nipple. He reads and rereads the same page. Tries reading the words in the chapter backwards from the end to the beginning, but the words keep tangling into naked men and their cocks in white sheets on the most comfortable bed in the universe.

At 3:00 a.m., Baxter shakes Templeton's shoulder. Templeton swings a meaty punch at Baxter, then wakes up.

Baxter settles himself onto the sofa in the half-light of the smoker, his knees curling up into his chest from a force greater than he can control, his face nuzzling and dribbling into the thin mattress while the wc door bangs open and closed, irregular and jarring.

Baxter dreams that the curled man who glowed like coal at the bottom of the linen locker has clawed a hole in the locker door with his fingernails and is crawling down the passageway, has crawled up to Baxter on hands and knees and closed his jaws on Baxter's ankle, the teeth clamping harder and harder through trouser leg, through sock, tooth squeezing and snapping bone. Baxter kicks the air, shaking the man off his leg, sitting up.

– Ouch! says Eugene, cupping his groin. – Watch what you're doing. You nearly kicked me in the baloney.

Eugene.

– Get up! says Eugene, windmilling his arms. – I need you to watch my car.

Eugene's suddenly speaking properly to him again!

– I can't, Baxter slurs.

– You've never been good for anything.

You've never been good for anything.

But that's a dream too. Baxter's eyelids flutter with exertion as he tries to pull them open.

– Loo, utters a voice.

Baxter leaps up, springing so high he's sure he touches the ceiling. Truly awake now.

Mad Mary sways in the doorway, out of his uniform and wearing rumpled nightclothes, clutching the door frame.

– Mr. Magruder! says Baxter.

Mad Mary wants to fire him for something, his knees dissolve, what did he do? He just might faint.

Mad Mary rocks from side to side, his hair every which way like flames from an exploded locomotive.

– Mr. Magruder? asks Baxter.

– I need to find loo.

– The loo?

– My pal Lou, says Mad Mary, and he gasps, tears gloss his eyes. – He's got leg bones sticking out of his chest, but that nurse with the three hairs on her chin told me not to worry. I want to marry her.

Mad Mary's skin is the colour of boiled fish, and he wipes his eyes with shaking hands, gasps, pokes at his eyes as tears leak, one of his fingers missing half a digit.

Mad Mary is a man returned from the battlefields of the Great War, returned with a fundamental derailment in his head. Edwin Drew was a returned man too. Served in the infantry and had a Victory Medal to prove it, the ribbon a startling rainbow.

– Oh, *Lou*, says Baxter.

Baxter scrutinizes Mad Mary's stunned, melted face.

– Where are we, Mr. Magruder? he asks.

– Hill 70, says Mad Mary, gasping through tears.

– All right, says Baxter. – Well, let's us go find a calmer hill.

– I want to go home.

– We'll get you home.

Baxter guides him to a car on the other end of the train to help him snuggle back into his berth, deep into the nest of his blankets.

DAY THREE
(WINNIPEG TO CALGARY)

Early morning, Templeton double-taps Baxter's forehead to wake him up. Baxter drags himself up to sitting in the half dark, his head dangling between his knees, then his palms pushing into his kneecaps. He crosses his arms and clenches his fingers and digs his fingernails into his forearms to wake himself up. He jolts to his feet, squeezes out fifteen squats before his bell rings and an arrow turns again for the berth ladder.

Hunched like a prawn, Baxter washes his furry teeth, his furry face, over a washbasin. Replaces his old shirt with a new one. In the mirror, strands of hair coil out behind his ears. He throws back his head, stretches out his back and arms to crack and crumble off the memory of the hard and narrow sofa bed. Then he stumbles through passageway after carpeted passageway to the diner for breakfast, stooped into the shape of a prawn again by the time he's closed the diner door behind him in the ruckus of the bouncing, jostling car. Eugene and Templeton sit folded over their plates, stabbing forks and knives through the food. Templeton's silvering hair trimmed clean at the back and sides, Eugene's eyes too big for his narrow face, just like Buster Keaton's except not the least bit comical.

– I don't believe you've got a famous writer in your car, Eugene says to Templeton.

Templeton digs a finger, mining for gold, into one of his small kidney-bean ears, the ears of a child stuck on the giant head of a man, while he tugs a fork's empty tines out of his mouth, chomps.

– Yes, I do, says Templeton through his food. – Fellow who wrote that book with the horse in it.

– So there *is* a famous writer? Baxter says, choking mid-bite on a spoonful of porridge, the cheapest item on the menu.

He coughs and heaves his choke, and his hands fly up to cup his mouth to catch oatmeal bits, but also to hide his flaring excitement. The porridge sprays into his mouth vestibule as he tries to swallow.

Templeton takes another bite and then sticks a finger back in his ear.

– Which book? Baxter asks.

Templeton smells wax bits on his finger, then brushes the ear wax away. – *Ride the Roaming?* Templeton asks the air, holding his fork up like a conductor's baton. – *Lasso the Lad?* Can't remember.

Eugene rubs an eye, mutters, then claps his hands in mid-air for no discernible reason.

– What's that? says Templeton. – You've got something to say?

Eugene shoves a forkful into his mouth. – Nothing, he says, chewing.

Eugene squeaks his fork tines through a tiny mess of codfish splatted on his plate. He goes back to muttering so much, Baxter can see masticated food plastering the surface of his tongue deep inside his mouth. But all the food clumps toward one side of his mouth. Eugene chews food on only one side of his mouth, suggesting he might have a decayed tooth. He should get that tooth extracted. Baxter would like to extract it.

Scraped-up porridge streaks the white of his bowl, but frankly not enough porridge. He wanted an egg, but it was too expensive. He spoons up the last bits of porridge, chewing through a wad of undercooked oats.

– What's his *name*? Baxter asks.

– What? asks Templeton.

– I said, what's the author's *name*.

– Julian Vine, Templeton says, clearing his throat and squinting as he leans in to sip from his coffee. – Now wait a second, Templeton says, holding up his hand to stop himself. – Maybe it was Jack Venable? Frederick Vellum? I forget. I had *things* to do, says Templeton. He laughs, but not in a joyous way.

– You're sure the last name starts with a V? asks Baxter.

– This isn't enough food, Eugene declares, pushing his chair away from the table, clapping his hands together again. – This is shameful. Martian's gnawing on raw porridge, I'm eating fish heads. It's yesterday's crumbs and scraps.

He hurls his napkin to the ground.

Baxter curls his toes inside his shoes. Eugene likes the word *crumbs*. He likes the word *workers*, he likes words like *union*, *brotherhood*, and *time and a half*. He's winding up for one of his political speeches, Baxter's seen it before, how his face squeezes up just before he speechifies, how his hands alternate between clapping and throwing open like he's at a pulpit, and he's going to spew in front of Templeton. Baxter needs to fly this chicken coop right *now*. He jams another spoonful of porridge into his mouth and chews like hell. Gulps coffee, scalds his palate and his tongue.

– We're grown men, says Eugene. – I'll be hungry in an hour. In half an hour. If I ate all three meals here I'd be out all the money I make in a day. A man cannot live only on the crumbs a greedy train company chooses to throw his way.

– Last name could be Vincent, come to think of it, says Templeton, scooping the last of his rubbery eggs into his wide mouth. It's more than enough breakfast, Eugene. *I'm* certainly full, he says, wiping his mouth with a napkin.

Baxter's never seen any stories by Julian Vine or Venable or Vellum in any table of contents in any magazine he's ever read. Or a Vincent. Count on Templeton not to remember one single, thrilling thing.

– Yeah, you're full, says Eugene. – You're full of Mad Mary's leftovers. And not feeding us properly is just one more way the company's swindling the workers. Even Martian here can understand it, can't you, Martian?

– The name's not Vincent, says Templeton, cocking his head with his mouth smiling but his eyes evil. Baxter dabbles his spoon in his bowl. Templeton and Eugene are fluffing their feathers, clawing the dirt. Eugene will lose, no matter what. – Do *you* understand what Eugene's saying, Baxter? asks Templeton.

– No.

– Maybe the name of the passenger *actually* starts with an E, says Templeton. – I believe it's an E. We work for the finest railway company on the continent, and indeed in the world. Correct, Baxter?

– E. E. Smith? asks Baxter.

– Yes, Smith! says Templeton.

– Who wrote *The Skylark of Space*? Baxter says, trying not to shout because what if it's true?

Templeton scrubs his mouth hard with his napkin. – What are your feelings, Baxter, about unions?

Eugene swivels his head to Baxter and scrunches his eyes. – Sky*what* of Space? What are you even talking about?

Templeton burps and stands up, tenting his fingers on the table. – I'm just fooling. I don't have a famous writer in my car. Just some regular old well-to-do sot who's drinking himself into an extortionate stupor.

– Who cares? says Eugene. – Space-story writers are all liars, cowards, and sissies anyway. Useless. Writing for little boys.

– A drunk passenger and a union-talking railman. Or union-talking rail*men*.

Templeton slides his eyes sideways at Baxter.

– Doesn't Eugene look just like Buster Keaton, says Baxter. – Like they could be twins.

He rushes the last of his coffee down his throat, the porcelain unyielding between his teeth no matter how hard he bites.

— WINNIPEG, THIRTY-MINUTE STOP. THIS WAY OUT PLEASE, announces Baxter.
— PLEASE CLAIM YOUR RIGHT BAGGAGE, he says.

He whisks jackets, brushes hats with his wooden brush as passengers detrain, bangs his shins and knees as he hauls suitcases out in the swirl and chattering hullabaloo of the Winnipeg train station, his knees only slightly jelly from the sudden landing on firm earth. Five dollars and sixty-five cents curled up in his palm, coins clanking down deep into his pocket. To his right, Templeton in his adjoining car fusses over his detraining passengers too, his smile juicier than it needs to be, his smile spilling into grovel that Edwin Drew would find contemptible. On Baxter's left, just one car past Freckles's, Eugene offers his hand to passengers without brushing down clothes or hats, as though he can hardly bother, his face rocky as Mad Mary marches toward him. Eugene slowly sets down a passenger's suitcase, and a Red Cap scoops it up as Mad Mary pulls Eugene aside by the arm. Baxter can't hear them over the clacks, screeches, and steaming of locomotives, shouts and calls from sellers, conductors, people hallo-ing detraining passengers or weeping them goodbye, but he reads Eugene's alarmed then furious Buster Keaton expression and he can smell the bitterness; to his right, poised next to his step box, Templeton grins wide and sated, his face as broad as the man in the moon's.

Baxter hauls away sacks stuffed with rolls of soiled linen, loads up with clean, he hands off telegrams and letters to Mad Mary. He trades coins for fried chicken and perogies from carts on the platform. Dinner tonight and lunch and maybe another dinner tomorrow.

He lived for a while in Winnipeg, near Sutherland. Where he rented a room from a Mrs. Lesiuk and her son Nicholas.

When he wasn't being shunted away on a train and called *George*, he gobbled books in his little room near Sutherland. He read and reread a calisthenics pamphlet, *Exercises for Healthy Men*. He knew all the photos by heart, the muscles, each calisthenic movement. He studied the hard muscled shoulders, curved thigh muscles. Some days he helped Mrs. Lesiuk carry in wood, haul coal, and carry her preserves up from or down into the cellar. Well, not *help*, precisely. *He* carried in wood while Nicholas Lesiuk smoked Pall Mall cigarettes under the apple tree and stared at him like he wanted to throttle him. Baxter didn't want to find another room to rent. Some lousy hotel close by the station. Another sad rooming house crammed with farting, snoring bodies in an attic or a damp and drafty great room. The bedbugs, rats, and mice.

Mrs. Lesiuk told him as he shouldered a basket of apples for her that Nicholas lost his job working at a delicatessen because police caught him smuggling liquor.

– I'm not embarrassed, she said, picking sweaty strands of hair away from her face. – Nicholas is a good boy. Beer is healthier than water.

Baxter could just picture it: Nicholas, cigarette hanging out of his mouth and eyes squinting in the tentacles of smoke, wrapping bottles of liquor up in butcher paper and scrawling on the side of the box, *Sausage*. Nicholas Lesiuk's teeth were wide-spaced and strong.

In the evenings Baxter rambled through the woods along the Assiniboine and Red Rivers, and then he closed the nights lying with his arm tucked behind his head on the neat little bed in Mrs. Lesiuk's house and memorized chapters in his battered copy of *The Practice of Dentistry*.

One of the last nights he spent at Mrs. Lesiuk's house, he finished his chapter early, so he tramped along the water, swatting away the mosquitoes. He jumped and squatted calisthenics in the woods, he recited the names of every tooth in the human mouth, one right after the other, in order. His favourites were the premolars.

He lingered longer that night, bursting his muscles, sweating, panting through his exercises.

Water oozed from the spongy ground as Baxter stepped among the trees and bushes, hopped over roots and knee-high ferns. He nearly collided with a few other solitary men out for walks in the dark, men doing private things, and his chest vibrated in panic for his own safety, a Negro man walking in the dark.

The red ember at the end of a cigarette nearly poked his eye out at the base of a tree. Nicholas Lesiuk.

– You, said Nicholas Lesiuk.

He blew cigarette smoke out the side of his mouth.

– Me, said Baxter.

They stood. Water in the river rushing and pooling along the bank.

– Well, said Baxter. – Good night.

– Good night, said Lesiuk, grinding out his cigarette.

And Baxter pushed back through the brush into the makeshift path he'd made behind him.

He was surprised Lesiuk was also out for a walk in the woods. Not surprised because Lesiuk seemed a strange, angry fool. He should journey back home before Lesiuk did.

He rambled through more tree and bush, his skin blooming like a flower, the rustles of small animals around his feet, an occasional bat silhouetted up high, the hoot of an owl, mosquitoes clustering to his exposed skin as he slapped at them.

Behind him, someone cleared their throat.

A tall man leaning against a tree. His skin an indeterminate colour in the dark.

Lesiuk had tracked him in the dark. Baxter curled his fists, ready to fight. Lesiuk strolled toward him.

– D'you have a match? whispered Lesiuk, a new cigarette in his fingers.

Baxter dipped into his pocket for a box of matches. Lesiuk took the match but didn't light his cigarette, just flipped the match back and forth around in his fingers, his breathing tight. Baxter held his breath, standing too close to Lesiuk, reading him, his nose in line with Lesiuk's chin, both giving the nod to their invisible contract. Lesiuk clenched his jaw, tucked the cigarette behind his ear, and leaned down and kissed Baxter square on the lips, their faces colliding, open-mouthed, starving. Men in the woods, men in laneways, are ravenous, silent creatures. Not that he had very much experience. Four times before Lesiuk. One other time in the woods, one time in a lavatory, two times in a laneway, always in the dark. Maybe some other times he didn't want to talk about.

Baxter's body lunged for every part of Nicholas Lesiuk, his tongue leaping into Lesiuk's mouth first thing so he could lick Lesiuk's teeth, his hard palate. They fumbled and groped each other's buttocks and cocks, clumsy. They kissed and pumped, moved their mouths and fingers and selves on each other, into each other, in their silence. Two figures flickering, then blinking out in the dark.

The high bushes, the water relentlessly lapping at the shores of the dark river.

They split apart as soon as they were done, slick and gasping, separating in the dark. Nicholas's unlit cigarette had moved from his ear and hung broken from the corner of his curled lips, his trousers slack as his long, lanky self receded back into the trees. Baxter's fingers silly and uncoordinated as he tried to button himself, tried to button down the glee. Lesiuk was a glorious, spindle-shanked man who smoked cigarettes in the woods along the banks of the Red River.

Now he *really* wouldn't sleep, his veins and arteries still steaming. He pulled up his blanket, pounded the flat pillow into a lumpy heap, trying not to think of Lesiuk's jiggling buttocks, the stretch of his chest and nipples, his long limbs folding and unfolding in the dark.

Baxter blew out the lamp, its flame blinking out. He lay in his mausoleum, in the dark, replaying sucking Lesiuk's cock. These rare, thrilling events, Lesiuk's skin pushed up against his skin, the two of them fused together with sweat and semen. The tongues and so much kissing, of cocks, of lips, the clashing of teeth. Sleep flirted with him, flitted close and flicked his nose, then flew away again. He recited all the permanent teeth in the human mouth to help him sleep, *third molar, second molar, first molar, second bicuspid, first bicuspid, cuspid, lateral incisor, central incisor, central incisor, lateral incisor, cuspid, first bicuspid, second bicuspid, first molar, second molar, third molar*, then started in on the occlusions, trying not to remember Nicholas Lesiuk or anyone else for that matter. *The upper central incisor is met in occlusion by the entire cutting edge of the lower central incisor and the mesial third of the cutting edge of the lower lateral incisor. The upper cuspid is met in occlusion by the distal cutting edge of the lower cuspid and the mesial two-thirds of the buccal* Lesiuk kissing the tip of his cock *cusp of the lower first bicuspid*. He punched and turned the pillow like a loaf of bread dough in Mrs. Lesiuk's hands as the night settled around him. *The upper first bicuspid is met in occlusion by the remaining ...*

Then he dropped into sleep like a cormorant plunging bill-first after a diving water snake. One of the best, longest sleeps ever experienced by a human on the entire planet Earth.

The next morning, Baxter's eyes clicked open of their own will, his head clear. He lay among the sheets, his body not his own, stunned at so much sleep, spittle caking the side of his mouth.

As he packed his bag, tucking in folded shirts that Mrs. Lesiuk had laundered, that he had ironed himself, he resolved to visit with Nicholas Lesiuk in the woods again the next time he was in Winnipeg. Mrs. Lesiuk had left meat-stuffed buns for him on the kitchen table. And coffee on the stove. As he ambled through the yard, Mrs. Lesiuk emerged from her tiny henhouse, eggs in her hands.

– You're leaving now?

– Yes.

– Nicholas is a good boy.

– Goodbye, Mrs. Lesiuk, he said. – Thank you for the excellent buns.

The light in Nicholas Lesiuk's room winked out.

The next time he did a layover in Winnipeg, Mrs. Lesiuk told him that Nicholas was in jail again. She swept the corners of the hallway, dug out beets and potatoes, silent.

Winnipeg.

This station nested in the Forks.

The passenger Punch and his red nose hover over his shoulder while the train stands in Winnipeg's Union Station, while Baxter clambers in and out of the train with bags of soiled linen that he exchanges for clean. Punch tails Baxter and asks him in seventeen different ways if the train will get to Sicamous on time, they are so looking forward to Sicamous and visiting with his sister, looking forward to days by the sea in Vancouver with even more of his family, his eldest brother's son a real joker, a superb swimmer too.

Judy's likely hounding Templeton or Ferdinand or Freckles.

Baxter offers his elbow to passengers as he helps them up into the train, Mad Mary evaporated from his duties, Baxter's smile broad but not too broad.

Among the passengers boarding stands a dimply blond lady bound for Section 5 without a companion of any kind, which worries him – she doesn't look like a sporting girl, her shoes burnished and the pattern of her dress lush and fitting like a lady's. She walks like a lady, a silk coat draped over her arm. She fingers a glistening barrette in her hair, cropped in a wavy bob, yellow and glinting, and clasped with a spider barrette, the spider studded with rhinestones or diamonds, perhaps. It's not like he can tell the difference between diamonds and rhinestones. She could be a spotter; that would explain a lady travelling alone. The last sporting girl he suspected he left alone. He shouldn't have left her to her own devices but he did, and she tipped him a perfumed dollar bill in the end.

Baxter helps the passenger with the glittering spider crouched in her hair up the steps, holds his breath in her whoosh of mothballs and medicine. She smells much older than her smooth dimples, her glossy hair, suggest.

The man curled up by the linen closet continues his trembling, his lips wide, his ember self, his teeth clamped. At one point Baxter opens the closet and the shelves stretch bare of linen, not a single stitch, not a fold, and his feet nearly give out under him, but then the linens fade back into view, grey, then white, blossoming in the dark, and filling out the shelves, obscuring the man and his troubles. Passengers saunter by, swinging bags, pocket watches, newspapers, Ethel Dell and Zane Grey books. Baxter steps over the man's glowing, discarded shoes in the vestibule, steps past him without even bothering.

Baxter settles the Spider into her seat, across from a wattly old businessman who flips a page in a folder without looking up. She rides against the train, upper berth.

– What a fine morning, she says to the businessman, her voice high and silvery. – I said, what a fine morning!

He digs his nose deeper in his folder and papers. She smiles at his rudeness as though her lips hurt, and pulls out a giant embroidery hoop that she picks at with her needle. The giant hoop wider than her bag, a magic feat indeed.

Two men in the same dun-coloured suits board, destined for Section 1, muttering to each other just long enough for Baxter to understand that they're in Pulp and Paper, and their report is due in two days, then a detailed budget two days after that. Paper reminds Pulp that he still needs to redo the numbers from Henderson.

– I said I'd get on it, says Pulp to Paper. – I said I would, didn't I? No need to get sore about it.

Paper grumbles and shifts his bulbous leather bag from his left hand to his right.

Compartment A boards. Baxter glances briefly at the face of the passenger booked in Compartment A, a scarf pulled up around the bottom of his face up to his nose, his hat pulled down low, his hair a stiff black, but his eyebrows, his eyelashes, so pale and blond he looks like he was formed out of blancmange. The hard soles of his shoes hammer the steps as he alights and plunges into the train. Baxter wonders if he just earned a demerit somehow, just for hearing those shoes louder than all the others.

Baxter offers his elbow to a spindly lady with curly grey hair spilling every which way, her mouth crammed full of teeth, sixty-four instead of thirty-two, multiple supernumerary teeth he is sure, as she tries to step up into the car holding a little girl by the hand. The girl's other hand grips a porcelain horse, the paint worn and flaked off about the muzzle and legs, one of the ears chipped. A Red Cap dumps their bags at the bottom of the steps.

– I see your friend's riding with you, observes Baxter to the little girl as he pats his forehead with a handkerchief in the sunny heat.

– Esme, says the lady, can you let my hand go for a moment? I can't lift you. Remember how Granny told you that her back smarts sometimes? Like needles when she has to pick up Esme?

She tries to pry Esme's fingers from hers.

Esme fights back silently, gripping her grandmother's hand like a starfish gorging on an oyster.

– Esme, please let go for a moment. Just one moment. Half a moment.

The old lady's face reddens, a drop of sweat slides out from under the brim of her hat, her coils of hair, and down her cheek.

– You step up, madam, he says, – and I'll lift her up after you.

He plucks the little girl from the bottom of the steps, her rib cage a bowl of bird bones. He floats her up alongside Granny as she balances on each step, trying not to trip, her captive hand choked in Esme's.

The granny's expression lies curiously flat. Esme jams her horse under her arm, swings round and grabs a hank of Granny's skirt, grabs Granny's hand.

Granny tries, one-handed, to navigate down the aisle, sort their things, settle them into their seats.

– Do you want to sit by the window, Esme? asks Granny. – So you can see outside better? You'll have to let go of my hand so you can sit on the other side. Then you can hold my other hand.

Esme's hand clenches.

Granny fixes on Baxter, seeing him, seeing through him.

– Her mother just passed, says Granny. – I am taking her to her father's family in Vancouver.

The Spider's head snaps in their direction.

Esme traces a lanky flower on her grandmother's jacket with one of her horse's spiky porcelain legs.

Baxter clicks on a smile. Helps passengers board, then settles their bags, wraps, and hats. Answers questions about the speed of the train, *Yes*, he says for the seven hundred and thirty-three thousand and fifty-eighth time, *the fastest train across the continent.*

As the train chugs and whistles out of Winnipeg and sets its sights on Saskatchewan, he chases after passengers who've just boarded, then he vigorously dusts the passageway walls to stay awake and stop the dusty prairies from infiltrating the car as passengers saunter in waves to the different lunch sittings. Finally he wilts to sitting on his stool in the smoker. Sleep pokes him in the ribs, he jostles, he jostles as the train huffs and sways its regular-irregular rhythm along the metal tracks, all aboard that invisible slurring of sleep, he tries to ignore its perpetual hammering, the bright sun prodding his eyes closed, only two more nights to go, grain elevators stuttering by on both sides of the train, the sun suddenly sharper, more abrasive. He sits, sleep clawing up his face. He fumbles his way to his locker and slips a perogy into his mouth whole and chews till it's gone. The postcard of naked men sits folded next to his heart. As the afternoon drags on, the bell chimes or a passenger flutters a hand at him, and he staggers to standing so he can fetch candy, crackers, sandwiches, and hear a passenger monologue an anecdote about their brother, their great-great-uncle, their automotive factory, their travels to Italy, China, Miami, Churchill, Nassau. Oh, and is the train running on time?

How would he know? He's not the damned engineer. He's not Father Time.

– Fastest train across the continent, he says, the sleep cogs in his brain whirring and smoking.

Baxter helps hunt for a wristwatch, a cigarette case, a woollen bunny also named Baxter, funnily enough, belonging to a child from an entirely different car.

And he sits. He sits and he sits and he sits and sits and sits. He sits. He steals snacks from his locker. Then he stands to survey the sections just in case. To at least put on the pretense that he's awake.

The Spider, embroidery hoop in her hand, needle sunk halfway in her fabric, sits mesmerized by Esme and Granny in their seat across the aisle. As Baxter passes by, she squeaks the needle through to the other side of the panel, then back up, but without looking away from Granny and Esme, the needle making arbitrary stabs and stitches. How is she capable of sewing without ever looking down? Judy, swaying through the aisle, stops next to the Spider.

– Do I know you? asks Judy.

Spider jolts in surprise and needles herself in the finger. She darts her bleeding fingertip into her mouth.

– Do I know you! retorts the Spider.

– I *know* you, says Judy.

Spider dabs at her finger with a handkerchief.

– Your photo is in my husband's magazine! You're famous.

Judy plops down beside the Spider. – How thrilling! Now what are you famous for precisely?

The wattly man across from them frowns; his business folders and papers stowed away, he's been thumbing through his bulky book about Napoleon, the book up close to his nose, and it seems these women are prattling too much, interrupting his time with the Emperor. He thumps the book closed, creaks to standing, and sways away with the rocking of the train.

In Broadview, Saskatchewan, the Spider and Judy detrain – *Just to stretch our legs on firm ground*, Judy says. The Spider and Judy swan around the platform briefly, Mrs. Tupper and her daughter following close behind, Judy chatting while the Spider nods, her hands behind her back, laughing or frowning appropriately.

As the women mount back up into the car, Judy asks Baxter amidst the hubbub, out the side of her mouth, – What laxatives do you carry aboard this train?

The locomotive hisses.

Mad Mary marches past Baxter with his ticket puncher. Neither of them mention Lou, neither mention Hill 70. They both only dreamt it.

As Mad Mary takes tickets during their brief stop in Broadview, Baxter nods at a passenger who introduces himself to Mad Mary, – Dr. Hubble, Professor of Medicine, he says. – Hold my bag, Porter, he tells Baxter.

Dr. Hubble, Professor of Medicine, backs up and takes a running leap toward the train, springing from the platform to the very top step. – Ta daaa! he says, and bows.

Baxter and Mad Mary clap politely. Baxter hands up the black bag to Dr. Hubble, Professor of Medicine.

Cigarette in hand in the smoker, Pulp of Pulp and Paper asks Baxter if he can sing, does he know any songs. Paper puffs on his pipe.

– Sadly, God did not see me fit enough to receive the gift of song, Baxter says.

– Well then, do a little dance for us, says Pulp, clapping his hands together, his cigarette peppering ash on the seat.

– I would, Baxter lies, – but I injured my foot in Toronto. Dropped a steamer trunk on my toe.

– What good are you then? asks Pulp, and Paper taps out his pipe into the ashtray and scrapes out the pipe bowl, keeping his face, suddenly pomegranate red, away from Baxter and focused on the pipe bowl, knocking and scraping it out over and over.

– Can't sing, can't dance, says Pulp, starting to laugh. – Can you pour a drink? Pulp chortles harder, spreads his legs wider in his seat.

– You already had four glasses of port at lunch, says Paper, standing up. – Let's get back to work.

– Ave Caesar, says Pulp, wrinkling his nose at Baxter as though they are friends, and he screws his cigarette into the ashtray.

Miss Tupper swaps her feathery hat for another feathery hat that tips forward in the front like a pirate's, up in the back like a ship's sail. A pink feather pompom swipes Baxter on the nose as she hops past him to her seat. The pompom pets him on the chin, and he swallows down a sneeze that nearly pops his brain out through his ears.

– Shouldn't you save that one for the honeymoon? asks her mother.

The mother, Mrs. Tupper, has hung her own hat on a hook by her head, and she pinches her lips in the tiny looking glass between the windows. A haze of toilet water, of silk, hangs around the women.

Baxter offers to hang Miss Tupper's hat on the hook by her head or put it in a hat bag, but she says, – No, I'll keep it on.

– It's stewing hot in here, says her mother, dabbing her own neck, her nose, the dip above her top lip with a handkerchief. – No need for a hat now that we're back on the train.

– It's new. I like it. You're the one who's hot.

Curly hairs stick to Miss Tupper's forehead. Mother and daughter start to argue about the lace trim on Miss Tupper's wedding-dress sleeves.

Judy plumps herself down across from the Spider. – What a day, she says. – I am in desperate need of a cup of tea. Would anyone like to come with me for a refreshing drink?

The Spider turns from Granny and her granddaughter to her sewing. She flips around her embroidery hoop, tugs at a knot the size of a boil, her ears also clearly perked by the Tuppers.

– You don't even like that hat, says the mother. – *Gerald* likes it.

– So?

– I don't mean, says Judy, – that *you* would have to drink a cup of tea if you didn't want to. You could have a lemonade.

– So, says Mrs. Tupper, – who marries a failing milliner? Who? I'd rather you were marrying a fishmonger. At least we'd get some haddock or halibut fillets out of it.

– You're just so unfair to him, says Miss Tupper. – He designed this one especially for me.

– Or a ginger ale? asks Judy, her varnished cheeks shinier and shinier.

Mrs. Tupper says, – Well, we'd understand him better if he could explain to us how his failing business is suitable for a man who wants to start a family.

– What does he need to explain? He makes *hats*.

Mrs. Tupper tugs at her bag under her seat. – Ugly hats, she whispers.

– Would *you* fancy a ginger ale? Judy asks Miss Tupper. – I heard a lady in the observation car say that there's a famous actor on this train. Do you know who it might be? Should we try to hunt him down?

– Porter, can you help me with my bag? asks Mrs. Tupper.

Baxter drags her bag out from under her seat. Is she carrying an anvil?

– No, says the Spider. – You go ahead.

The Spider's needle hovers high in the air above her sewing as she leans toward the Tuppers' scuffle.

– Well, I guess I'll go on my own then, says Judy. – I'll be lonely. Maybe I'll see the extremely famous actor. Would be a shame to do that by myself.

But Judy stays perched on her seat across from the Spider.

– Well, Mrs. Tupper says, digging out of her bag small boxes, fluffy lacy things, magazines, a *Farmer's Almanac*, two cast-iron bookends shaped and painted like pink pigs, and book after book after book, – you're going to have to take that hat off to sleep, Carlotta. That's just plain fact. I look forward to seeing your head one day, seeing as how I haven't seen you without a hat for a good three days.

She snaps closed the bag. She opens one of the books to a bookmark pasted with pressed purple pansies and smooths the open pages.

– We'll see, says Miss Tupper. – Father said he didn't want you drinking liquor. He even said –

– It was just a cocktail! Besides, the rules are different on trains. Isn't that right, Porter?

– That's what some folks say, madam, says Baxter.

– Ha! says the mother. – See? What did I tell you? The rules of the railroad. Your father can suck an egg.

She peeks into the mirror in their section and pats a curl on her temple. – I'm ready to throw that hat out the window. All this *Gerald* stuff. Gerald does this and Gerald thinks that. You didn't invent engagement, you know. Porter, can you help me open this window a little? A few people in this world have actually gotten engaged before. Marriage doesn't make you *special*. I was engaged and then a newlywed once too, you know. You're the queen of your wedding for a day, maybe two, and then when the wedding's done, nobody cares and you're stuck for the rest of your life and all eternity with *Gerald*. Or in my case your father. Gerald hasn't read a single book in his stodgy, young-fogey life, I'd wager.

– Gerald has.

– *Gerald has*, the mother parrots, winking at Baxter. – *You* used to read books. You used to love them.

Baxter tugs open the window, tempted to jump out of it, his fingernails grating against the sill. Should he be worried about the wink? The postcard rests against his rib cage.

– Who cares? Miss Tupper says. She pats the pompom, fluffs it. – There are other things in life besides *books*. Gerald says novels are just lies and distraction.

– Well then, Gerald can suck an egg too, says her mother, and Baxter wedges the bag in tighter under the seat, then jumps back.

– Porter, how much longer until we reach Banff? asks Miss Tupper. – Are we almost at Banff yet?

Baxter says they should reach Banff by 10:55 a.m. tomorrow, but Miss Tupper's already turned back to her mother.

– You just want to write about it, don't you? says Miss Tupper to her mother. – In one of your *stories*.

– My *stories* paid for your finishing school. My *stories* pay for your nice clothes, your nice house, your nice holidays, your wedding to *Gerald*. Do you think your father's wages could pay for the dinner? Lounging around in gentlemen's clubs doesn't pay any bills. What time is dinner, Porter? asks Mrs. Tupper.

– You're an *author*, says Judy, leaning toward them. – I'm sorry to have been eavesdropping.

The Spider leans over Judy's shoulder, her barrette glinting. – Anything I might have read? Under what name?

– She writes romance novels, says Miss Tupper.

– *Thyme and Sage*, says Mrs. Tupper. – *Nutmeg and Cinnamon. Cloves and Cardamom.*

– Oh, the Hiram Hart novels! How exciting, exclaims Judy, her mouth opening wide, so wide Baxter can see her uvula, remarkable. – You're Hiram Hart! I am also thinking of writing a novel.

Miss Tupper crosses her arms, tosses herself back on her seat.

– What time is dinner, Porter? asks Mrs. Tupper.

– First sitting is in an hour and a half, he says.

– You're not *already* hungry? asks Miss Tupper, fanning herself.

– Porter, says Mrs. Tupper. – I would like a glass of raspberry wine.

– You know father doesn't like it.

– I'm always thirsty, her mother says. – You know that.

She turns to Baxter.

– That glass of raspberry wine.

– Porter, says Miss Tupper, turning to her mother, – I want a Hanky-Panky.

Her mother's face flashes bright red.

– I'd love a biiiiig Hanky Panky.

Carlotta Tupper reaches a fifty-cent piece up toward him. He can't take the tip. The rules! He clenches his teeth so hard he hears a crack.

– A fifty-cent tip! says the mother. – *Someone* thinks she's Consuelo Vanderbilt!

As he recommends they go to the club car for drinks, *The view so much better, Mrs. and Miss Tupper, alcohol can only be consumed in the club car*, Mad Mary materializes at his elbow.

Mad Mary hands a telegram to Miss Tupper. – Missed you the first time around, Miss, he says.

– And a letter for you, madam, he says, handing an envelope to Mrs. Tupper.

Then he skips off, jaunty and well-rested.

– Oooh! I'm sure it's from Gerald. Lovely, says Miss Tupper, fondling the telegram in its envelope. She holds it up to her nose and breathes it in. – I'll open it later as a present for myself. He said he'd let me know where the honeymoon will be as a surprise.

Mrs. Tupper shreds open her envelope and reads the single sheet of paper inside. She folds it back up, quickly, crookedly, and rams it into the final pages of her book.

– Any happy news you can share? asks the Spider abruptly, her hoop held loose in her hands.

– No, says Mrs. Tupper, tucking her book under her arm, and then standing up and straightening her skirt. – Carlotta, let's go to the solarium to see the view, she says. She holds out her hand to Miss Tupper.

– What? asks Miss Tupper.

– I would really like to see the view.

– Look! says Miss Tupper, not standing, pointing out the window. – A black-and-white cow!

She taps on the glass.

She scowls at her mother. Then she titters on about how the telegram is sure to be some surprise from Gerald, such a lovely, thoughtful fellow, maybe about their honeymoon. – I still don't know where we're going for our honeymoon, she tells Judy, who bobs her head like the marionette she is.

– It's going to be a surprise, says Miss Tupper. – I hope it's Venice.

Mrs. Tupper crosses her arms. – I will be in the solarium, she says. – Carlotta, I will wait for you there.

– No!

Miss Tupper spins her head from the window, to her mother, to Judy, to the Spider. She crosses her arms and crosses her legs because she's not going anywhere. The telegram tumbles from her lap. The Spider darts toward the telegram, as though hoping to magically read through the envelope.

Baxter leaps after the telegram and offers it to Carlotta Tupper. She doesn't look at him as he passes it to her, just holds out her hand like the princess-and-the-pea that she is.

– I'll take that telegram, says Mrs. Tupper.

– No! says Carlotta. – Why are you being such a tyrant? I don't want to speak to you today.

– Fine, says Mrs. Tupper. – I'll let you find out by yourself.

She takes her book from under her arm, holds it in both hands, and charges away down the aisle.

– Find out what! calls out Miss Tupper.

He retreats to the passageway alongside the compartments, puts his ear to Compartment A's door. So far the bell for Blancmange's compartment has remained unrung. Baxter whips out a cloth and fights the dust germinating before his very eyes on the panels, the light fixtures, while the green-and-tan fields of grain whip past, the occasional herd of cattle, farmhouse, the landscape belching dust and growing more and more hilly by the mile as they near Alberta. Once, he wobbles from sleepiness. Only once. His eyelids scrape across his eyeballs with every blink.

He might be seeing things, because while he polishes the brass rail along the wall, a preternaturally dowdy, spectacled woman with black hair exits Blancmange's compartment and barrels past him, her head down.

Baxter wipes his glasses with a cleaning rag instead of his hand-kerchief, and when he puts them back on, he sees nothing but blur.

He surveys the sections. The Tuppers have evaporated, probably bickering and daring each other to drink turpentine in the solarium. The Spider no longer sits in her seat, but has migrated and rooted herself beside the child Esme and Granny. Her hands empty and red without their embroidery. Judy leans into the small party too.

– I understand the little girl's mother recently passed away, says the Spider, tipping her head sympathetically.

Granny nods.

– Well, the Spider says in her tinkly voice, – I know this might be forward of me, but I am quite famous. Perhaps you've heard of me? My name is Mrs. Sarah Crane from Boston and I have recently been conferencing with fellow spiritualists in Winnipeg. There was a feature written about my powers as a medium in a prestigious science journal. Through my spirit control, I am able to speak with the dead –

Baxter leaps forward faster than the fastest train.

– Littlegirldoyouwannaseethetrain'sengine?! Baxter says.

He grabs Esme's other hand and yanks her away, her granny's veiny hand naked, free. The flesh still bloodless from where Esme has been choking it.

Baxter stops his breath. He hangs suspended underwater, drowned and drifting thousands of leagues beneath the sea. These white ladies, this tiny child with her tiny head, her short scraps of hair, peering at him from out of the porthole of their submarine window, their faces twisting in fascination, souring into revulsion.

Esme's other hand snatches at his thumb. Her ten pale fingers clamp tiny and damp on to his large bony hand, anemone tentacles.

– Yes please, she says.

– We will hold a séance, says the Spider.

– How stupendous! says Judy, her mandible clacking open then closed, and the jewelled droplets in her earlobes quivering.

Granny's lips compress with disapproval.

Baxter hoists Esme onto his hip and gallops her away to the front of the train, her raccoon-sized hands steel grips around his neck.

Of course the Spider's just finished attending a conference in Winnipeg. Damned Winnipeg spiritualists. Next the Spider will be asking for random objects and furniture, an inordinate number of candles, a table with three legs, something ludicrous like that, and he'll no doubt have to worry about them setting the car on fire or gouging the panelling. They'll try to disturb the dead. He can't stand it when passengers try to fool with the dead. Aunt Arimenta always said that the dead are all around us, but that doesn't mean you need to strike up a conversation with them. On the island it was nothing to talk about the spirits walking, to dream of the dead sometimes, not like here where talking about the dead is the province of charlatans and swindlers holding their hands out for money. The Spider will be asking for money any second now. Where's Harry Houdini, Master Mystifier, when you need him? Maybe Baxter should tell Mad Mary. No. The Spider will get him fired. Just like Eugene. The little girl will get him fired.

Only two more nights.

Behind the curtain at their rabbit stew dinner.

Templeton's still laughing to himself, his wide mouth open and joyous, and his milky tongue exposed for all the world to see, because *of course* a famous writer isn't on the train. Freckles spends a minute sprinkling a soup spoon full of salt on his bowl of stew, his freckles shedding into his stew and peppering the table. Then he paddles his spoon in his stew, looking for any scraps of meat among the bones and potatoes.

– Charles Dickens ain't either, he says. – And Tom Mix got his times mixed up and forgot to get on at Kenora, ha ha!

Freckles laughs.

– I have a famous writer in my car, says Baxter.

– Who? Templeton frowns.

– Hiram Hart, says Baxter. – Say, do any of you know an Edwin Drew? A porter who used to work for the company?

Templeton guzzles from a glass of water, irritated. – Hiram Hart's not that famous. I heard there might be a famous actor among us, travelling incognito. Anyone know anything about that?

– Never heard of an Edwin Drew, says Freckles, sweat glossing his upper lip. – Who's Hiram Hart?

Templeton chews, Freckles chews, the train rocks.

Baxter takes a bite of gristle, chews. – What happened to Eugene? Was he fired?

Templeton and Freckles study the food in their bowls.

Ferdinand plops out of nowhere into Eugene's seat, setting down a plate of toast and gravy. Ferdinand! Has he brought his kite on this run?

– So much to do, says Ferdinand. – Hello, fine gentlemen! Freckles, my friend! Templeton, sir! I have five minutes to eat. Tops.

– Ferdinand! says Baxter, and he leaps up to shake his hand. – I saw you earlier but you were too far away.

– Why, joyful salutations, my friend, says Ferdinand, pumping Baxter's hand in a hearty shake.

– What about Eugene? Baxter asks the table. – How's he going to feed his kids?

Templeton rips a roll in half.

Freckles ducks his head, spooning stew into his mouth too quickly, trying to end this meal as soon as possible, flinging sweat drops as he gulps down the hot stew in the hot summer night.

Baxter's brain feels like it's been kicked.

– Excuse –, he says, swallowing down the *me* as he rushes away from the table.

– You need to eat more, says Templeton, hollowing out his bowl.

The trembling man who was curled up in the linen closet now huddles in a corner of the vestibule. He calls to Baxter, his lips opened wide, his body glowing, and a sick humidity descends on Baxter. He lays his hands on the door to his car, propping himself up. He stands there for too long, the floor, the walls, shifting around him, trying to buck him off. He opens the door to his car and pulls himself inside. He slams the door behind him.

Kuzyk calls out as he strides down the passageways, down the aisles, *First call for dinner!*

Pulp and Paper in their matching suits bustle up to him. – Porter, says Pulp, Pulp in front. – We need our berths ready when we get back.

Paper whistles a non-song, hunts for a non-thing in his pocket, refusing to look Baxter in the eye.

Baxter descends on their section as quickly as a vulture tearing at a carcass, snapping the seats together to make the lower berth, unlocking the upper berth, swiftly unfolding, smoothing, and tucking sheets and blankets.

He's plumping the first pillow when they abruptly re-materialize behind him, pie crust crumbing their faces.

– You're still not done, George? asks Pulp, his words slurring. – You're bloody slow.

– Just five more minutes, sir, says Baxter. *Click click.*

– You're too bloody slow, George, says Pulp, *click click click.* He turns to Paper. – Want to play bloody cards?

– I *want* to go to bed, says Paper.

– But I'm not tired. You're a bloody old farty fart. Let's play bloody cards. Let's get a bloody drink.

– Perhaps you might try the solarium, gentlemen, says Baxter. – Watching the sun set is quite lovely indeed, and one of the finest features of this train.

Baxter keeps making down the beds for Pulp and Paper as they mutter and dodder, then mutter back from where they came, Pulp still cursing *bloody* this and *bloody* that as if no ladies ride this train.

Mother and daughter Tupper trip off to dinner, Mrs. Tupper swathed in satin, trailing a sulphurous wind she breaks as she passes by him.

Rotten people.

Rotten train.

He has a postcard in his pocket. The sheets start to foam under his hands. The foam creeps up past his wrists, up to his elbows, spills down the front of his trousers. He closes his eyes.

Sleep.

Steam hisses and brakes squeal as the train briefly slows, then resumes speed.

– Right on the button, says Punch, materializing behind Baxter, too close. – We've arrived exactly on the second!

His carved face twitching with glee. Judy gleams back, her eyelids snapping open and closed.

The train steams past a flock of sheep.

Baxter asks other passengers if he's permitted to break down their berths and can they please gather their personal effects. He chases an escaped spool of embroidery thread belonging to the Spider. He glimpses the panel she's embroidering on her hoop. Loose loops of thread and patches showing the fabric underneath, is that a turnip or a cloud?

He breaks down berth after berth, seats snapping into place, panels clicking down, as more passengers saunter off to dinner.

Dr. Hubble, Professor of Medicine, salutes Baxter as he heads in the direction of the diner. – Greetings! he says.

Baxter whirls around to see to whom Dr. Hubble might be speaking.

– Greetings to *you*, says the doctor.

– Good evening, Dr. Hubble, says Baxter.

– A good evening to you too! says Dr. Hubble. He saunters away.

Punch stands, chest puffed up, at the end of the passageway, immensely proud of the time, fingering his gleaming watch like it's a rare gold doubloon, fields undulating outside the windows as the train races though them. Grain elevators studding the yellowing fields of grain as the dying sun slumps down into the horizon. The sun setting practically in the middle of the night, this part of the country.

Blancmange in Compartment A hasn't rung him for anything since he boarded this morning in Winnipeg. And the only person Baxter's seen exit is the dowdy lady who might have been figmental, she's so unlike the other people who ride this train.

Baxter rings the buzzer of Compartment A. Blancmange opens the door – his blond eyelashes, blond eyebrows – then throws himself onto one of the seats and plasters his face against the window, his nose and forehead flattened, his pale hair ruffled. The window sports multiple grease shadows, each one in the shape of a man's face. This man's face.

– This is around the time I would normally make down your bed, sir, says Baxter.

– I'm fine, mumbles Blancmange. – Can you please close the door either in front of you or behind you? I don't want strangers poking their heads in.

God*damn*it. The compartment stinks of whisky.

– I can bring you a brandy ... Should I find a doctor –

– No, he says. – I'm fine. I'm just keeping to myself.

The train whistles.

Baxter closes the door. Studies the glimmering striations and whorls in the polished wood grain, fingernail-thin inlay in the form of wild rose petals. Grinds his teeth first in one direction. Then the other. A grinding echo.

Blancmange had better not vomit.

– We are not one minute ahead nor behind schedule, announces Punch over Baxter's shoulder. – Regina was right on time.

His red mouth smiling like a freshly laid egg in the nest of his pointed beard. – My sister will be so pleased. What a feat of modern machinery this train is!

– Fastest train across the continent, sir, says Baxter.

Punch jingles the chain of his pocket watch, snaps it closed, and continues jaunting down the passageway.

He reminds Baxter of the tartness of applesauce. Baxter's stomach would not flinch at a bowl of applesauce.

Back on the hopper, fields speeding by and the train speeding into night, his hands unfold the postcard, straighten and smooth it out on his knee. Who are these men, coiled together on the postcard? How did the men feel putting their hands and mouths on each other like that? Did they like it? How this card in his palms could get him dismissed immediately. Or put in jail. His hands cupping the edges, he can't drop it down the hopper just yet.

He wants to know where in Winnipeg Eugene ended up, and what obscenities Eugene shouted – of course he must have shouted, Eugene not a taciturn man – when the superintendent told him he was dismissed. Eugene is probably still shouting obscenities, cursing and crackling the air an electric blue.

Baxter's breakfast, lunch, and dinner bubble, rise, and spew out his mouth.

As the locomotive drags its load through Saskatchewan, Blancmange estivates in his Compartment A, and Baxter's board still hasn't yet rung, summoning him to Compartment A to fetch a snack from the diner or to break down the berth. It's the middle of the night, they're probably crossing into Alberta now, he can't tell in the dark, and tomorrow before noon they'll arrive in Banff. Baxter cuffs the cloudiness off his watch face. Not having broken down Blancmange's compartment itches at his ribs, makes him squirm.

He opens the shoe locker belonging to Blancmange's compartment, and Baxter extracts a pair of lady's shoes. Green uppers with high, generous heels. Blancmange *has* stowed a lady with him, the dirty cad! And she's getting her green shoes shined too! Baxter ties the green ribbon laces so she'll know he's shined the shoes, he knows she's stowed away in there, and the nefarious stowaway and her beau know he knows that they know, and pretty soon Mad Mary will know too.

Or he can pretend he hasn't noticed. He can't risk demerits.

How much food, how many sandwiches, could Blancmange have possibly packed to eat with his illegal lady love in his expensive Compartment A, and how much blame will Baxter get if Blancmange faints from hunger or dies of starvation? Where was she? She must be hiding in the WC. She must somehow be smuggling food back to him from the diner. Baxter refuses to worry; if Blancmange wants to melt away into nothing but a stain, why should Baxter care, just one fewer pair of shoes to shine, and judging from what he saw of the shoes on his feet, Blancmange's filthy shoes probably cost two hundred dollars, so Blancmange will never run out of food because he could just sell his shoes.

Baxter sways for a few seconds with the rocking of the train outside Compartment A. He cannot argue his way into the room of course. He's also not sure if he's glad or sad. Glad because it's one fewer bed and passenger to deal with, the passenger isn't sick, or sad, because he's obviously dealing with a stiff, *two* stiffs, and now he'll lose out on a tip, sad because Blancmange and this woman are probably up to some kind of eccentric, wealthy-people hijinks, sad because he'll probably have a secret, squirrelly mess in there for him to clean up once they reach Vancouver.

During his porter training, Edwin Drew told him and the other students about porters happening upon dead bodies in the middle of a run. A barrister who died of a heart attack in the smoker when all the passengers had gone to bed. Edwin Drew, trying to wake him from his nap. The heaped meatiness of his face, the gaping mouth, and Edwin Drew momentarily stuck in time, his brain an empty cave.

Edwin Drew paused, and the student porters all held their breaths.

Was finding a dead passenger in the manual? Edwin Drew had asked himself. Not that he could recall. He yanked open his instruction book, he said, riffled through it in a ridiculous frenzy, and of course found nothing. The dead man's limbs hardened with rigor mortis in the smoker, and the best thing Edwin could do was tell the conductor and make it the conductor's problem so that he was not the only one cringing when the man's head accidentally clunked against the door frame as they tried to angle his sheeted body out the door.

Right now, Baxter hovers outside Compartment A. He will not suffer this stowaway scandal by himself.

Baxter turns tail to find Mad Mary. What choice does he have?

Mad Mary's larking around with Templeton, each man digging in his own ear as they gossip. – I'll be by in a minute, says Mad Mary, as he corkscrews an eardrum with his little finger.

Baxter plants himself back on his stool with the green ladies' shoes in the smoker. On his pocket watch, the minute curdles into an hour, two hours, past midnight. The doorway hangs empty.

Out of nowhere, a woman with hair the colour of a dirty mop and a matching dress bullets past the doorway, her head down.

He accidentally scrubs the green shoe with his handkerchief. In the rattling murk of this submarine, Baxter drifts back and forth, collects shoes lined under the berths, tucked into lockers, soaps numbers and letters on the soles, snaps out a cloth over his knees. He gives up on polishing only two pairs at a time. He digs in to the rotten, leathery pile.

He buffs leather uppers. Again and always. His container of brown shoeshine has only a few smears left. He'll have to borrow some from Freckles. He imagines Templeton probably charges for every smear of shoeshine. Freckles pops into the darkened doorway.

– Going down, he says.

– Going down?

– See you on the other side, God willing.

2:07 a.m. He sits on the hopper again, his only escape, staring into the dark hole between his legs as rail ties blur by in the dark. He misses standing still.

The train shunts between somewhere and something.

He grips the postcard between his fingers. He longs so much for the tousled bed, for the men locked in the postcard, his skin hurts, stretches too tight; a space inside his chest concaves and takes shape, rears up and bangs against the bars of his rib cage.

Years ago, he can't remember when, he clung to the trunk of a great cedar in Vancouver, his arms grasping its trunk. He ground his chest into its rough skin, the salty water of the bay licking the shore, starfish suckering the rocks, a man shaped like a starfish suckered onto him, water shaped like a man licked him salty. Ghosts in the woods bordered by saltwater. Baxter, a Negro man wandering silent in the woods, picking his way through bushes and dripping ferns.

He tries not to think about the starfish that live in all kinds of forests, of trees, of buildings. He is addicted like a dope fiend, his hands clasping starfish buttocks in the damp and lethal trees, the mist. Baxter solid as a tree.

He tries not to look at the faces. In the bushes and trees and laneway, in the dark, he doesn't even try. But he knew the Polish milkman in Regina by the slightly hunched posture. Nicholas Lesiuk in Winnipeg. The Squamish fellow in Vancouver. They all feasted on each other, sometimes for whole minutes, sometimes only seconds. He's never seen another trainman haunting the bushes and trees. Once he thought he did, but he had mistaken a shadow for himself, the shadow of a shadow. Always in the dark.

When all candles be out, all cats be grey.

He hopes.

That time he fell out of the woods and onto the streets. A chicken pecked at crawling things in the grass. A dead dog simmered on the street, waiting for the garbage collector to gather it up, its mangy legs splayed, doing a circus trick.

His bell rings.

The tiny girl Esme surveys him while clamped to Granny's hip, an arm wound around Granny's throat, the other arm clenched around the torso of her chipped porcelain horse, her face as impassive as Granny's.

– She's not sleeping, says Granny, her voice gritty with exhaustion, her hair spilling out one side of her boudoir cap, her eyes puffed. – I am at my wit's end, Porter. Surely you must know of some trick to calm her down.

Esme butts and burrows her head into Granny's neck.

Baxter holds out his arms. He remembers what his aunt Arimenta always said when she wanted to calm him down when he was boy.

– The planet Saturn has more than one moon, he says.

Esme sticks a horse leg in her mouth and clamps it with her teeth. Granny squints.

He fixes his eyes on Esme's as though there is nothing else and no one else in the world, the galaxy, the universe: – Esme, I know the names of Saturn's moons: Titan, Iapetus, Rhea, Dione, Tethys, Mimas, Enceladus, Hyperion, and Phoebe.

– Mmm hmm, Esme says.

– I could teach you the names too, he says.

She unwinds her arm from Granny's neck, hugs the horse to her chest with both hands. Granny sets her down on the floor, and Esme keeps hugging her horse.

Granny crawls into her berth and yanks the curtain closed behind her. She gusts out a snore before Esme and Baxter even reach the end of the aisle.

Esme sits on the floor of the smoker, planted in the puddle of her nightgown as he shines shoes and whispers the names of Saturn's moons. He gives her a clean cloth and lets her brush and polish her horse, the brush gigantic and clumsy in her hands. He passes her one of his shoes to buff, his socked foot tapping. Exaggerated recesses around her eyes hollow out her face. She runs the brush up a shoelace.

They return the pairs of shoes in the half-light, her trotting behind him, and once the shoes are all tucked away, he lays out playing cards between them on the sofa.

– Your turn, says Freckles, rounding the edge of the doorway.

Freckles stops short in the smoker doorway.

– Do you want to join us? asks Baxter.

– N, O means no, says Freckles, dashing away.

Every so often when Baxter blinks, he has a thimble-sized dream. One about a radish sprinkled with salt. Another in which he rides astride an ant. Esme does not lie down to sleep, even when he pulls out the mattress and plops her on top of it, wraps her in his blanket; like a gecko she doesn't even seem to blink. They turn the cards face down, they turn them face up, they sort them into red and black, they sort them into matching numbers, they flutter out a round of Old Maid, then they build little houses that slide apart with every small jerk of the train.

Baxter yawns. Scratches the back of his neck.

When the bell chimes, she trails behind him, holding on to the back of his jacket as he moves the ladder, as he brings another pillow for Mr. Pulp, of Misters Pulp and Paper, who scrambles down for a trip to the WC.

Granny rouses in a white dressing gown around 4:00 a.m., her hair tucked back up in its cap. – Esme, she says, holding out her hand. – Come to Granny.

Esme matches a two of clubs with a two of spades, her face down.

Granny stands in the smoker doorway in her dressing gown, her body rigid even as it rocks with the movement of the train. She turns and creaks back into the dim.

– Who's this little lady? Templeton asks when Baxter seats himself at breakfast, Esme climbing up onto his lap.

Esme fiddles with one of Baxter's gold buttons and mumbles into his chest.

– That's a pretty interesting name, Mmmmblmmblm, says Templeton.

Esme throws her head back and lets out a single, gravelly laugh from her dry lips. She burrows her head back into Baxter's chest and curls her horse Rocky up under her chin.

– How are you doing this fine morning, Baxter? asks Templeton, catching up his cup of coffee.

– Sleepy, says Baxter.

Templeton laughs. – Yes, he says.

Templeton sets down his coffee, marches away, and then marches back with two plates of raisin toast. He sets the plates down in front of Baxter.

– One for Miss Mmmmblmmblm, says Templeton, – and one for you.

– Thank – thank you, says Baxter.

– You're welcome, says Templeton. He sips his coffee. He looks down at his dirty plate, and his smile slips away.

Baxter wishes he knew the right thing to say so they could all stop being so tired.

Esme gnaws at the crust of her freshly buttered raisin toast. Baxter also bites into his piece of freshly buttered raisin toast, and savours the hot fruit bursting on his tongue.

After breakfast, Baxter paces up and down the passageway, hoping Esme might sag into sleep with the monotony, curled in his arms.

As he drags his feet across the long stretch of carpet, he has a fruitfly-sized dream that he's lying in a field in late summer, long grass, the sun twinkling, and Eugene Grady in his straw hat bumps his bicycle up and over Baxter's stomach on his way to buy Pall Malls.

That he steps into the jewel-blue ocean back home on the island. No, a brilliant emerald lake in the Rockies. His feet turning into grouper tails, then beaver tails, under the water.

He stumbles, clutching Esme's head like a coconut so he won't drop it. She climbs, wide awake, up onto his shoulders. The bell rings.

He hustles back and forth, replenishing towels, wiping up slops. Passengers wiggle their fingers hello at her on his shoulders as they zip through their libations.

– Hello, young lady! chirps the Spider, her barrette glinting.

Baxter trips. A porcelain horse's hoof bumps into the crown of his head as he splashes his palms against the wall and catches himself.

Esme wails when Granny scoops her away.

– You can wear the dress with the yellow flowers, says Granny, trailing a bawling Esme behind her.

He sways, deranged with lack of sleep, fire licking at the edges of his brain.

Dr. Hubble, Professor of Medicine, salutes Baxter as he strides down the passageway to the diner, does a pirouette just before he rounds the corner, and collides with the wattly man who drops his biography of Napoleon, the pages fluttering, the dust jacket flipping off. Baxter dives for the book. The exposed cloth cover is not the title of a biography of the Emperor Napoleon. It's *Lady Audley's Secret*. Baxter hands the book back to the man, who growls away back in the direction from which he came.

The train rumbles into Medicine Hat station. Esme tucks herself into a corner in the vestibule, a tiny shadow shrouded in a yellow-flowered dress, while Baxter steps outside, then back inside, helping a passenger detrain and welcoming another aboard. He catches his toe on the step box only once.

That morning, Esme helps him deliver a slopping glass of mineral water for Mrs. Tupper, a small bag of peppermint humbugs for Granny that Esme partially spills, a small shower of humbugs bouncing on the carpet, but Granny shows her supernumerary tumble of teeth in a wince that passes as her version of a smile.

– I want to be a porter when I grow up, says Esme, and the shouts of laughter from the passengers nearby ring so loudly Baxter can't hear anything else, he certainly can't hear the car rumbling over the tracks for a good few seconds. Granny rubs a pearled earlobe with a shrivelled finger. Baxter glances out the window at an aproned woman standing in among yellowing blades of grain, straight as a blade of grain herself, oozing and waiting forever as the train rumbles by. The woman leaps for the train and her fingers start clawing up over the windowsill as she tries to clamber in through the window.

– Excuse me, madam, he says to Granny, and he lifts the fingers one by one away from the sill. – Just an insect, he says.

Granny tut-tuts over Esme. The aproned woman dissolves back into the blades of grain.

The aproned woman belongs to the mysterious sleepy clan. All Baxter needs to do is sleep properly and the clan won't appear. Aunt Arimenta always told him not to worry about them. *Important as dust*, she'd say. *Now close your eyes, try to sleep.*

– Porter, asks Granny, – what kind of grain is in that field?

– Wheat, he says. He has no idea.

Passengers' bursting smiles trail him and his Esme-remora wriggling alongside him. Sometimes he just lifts Esme up in his arms and works one-handed, or he lets her hang off his back, her skinny legs and arms coiling around him.

She grips his hand, his legs, his arms. Her arms tighten around his neck, her legs clamp around his waist. When he carries her, hanging like a rucksack, to Granny's section and leans backward so she can step down to the floor, she suctions to him harder and tighter the closer he comes to Granny.

– Granny misses you, he says, talking to the mass barnacled to his back. – She wonders where you've gone all morning.

– Come, Esme, says Granny, pulling Esme's elbow, – let me read you some Mother Goose. Or *Children of the Old Testament*? We like that one. I've got your horse. I've got Rocky.

Esme fingers strangle his Adam's apple. She kicks her foot out at Granny.

– Come get Rocky.

– If you play with your Granny now, says Baxter, – I'll tell you a story later about a boy and a girl named Hansel and Gretel. That's a good one.

He crouches down and leans back so she can climb down onto the floor, but instead she climbs around his torso to his front, and he grabs her with his arms.

– I already know that story, says Esme, her face crumpling and pinching, clasping on to Baxter more tightly while batting away Granny's hand in stringy fervour. – Mama told me that story.

Esme whispers, her voice staccato-ing the syllables as she bangs her forehead against the gold buttons of Baxter's jacket, – Mama told me *all* the stories I already know all the stories I know every story I know every story Mama's telling me stories –

Granny's mouth falters and trembles as she grips a tiny slip of Esme's dress hem between her knobbly index finger and thumb, the only part of Esme's person Esme doesn't bat her away from. Other passengers pivot their faces away from the spectacle, hinge their faces down into their magazines and books, toward weeds, animals, grain elevators racing outside the car windows. Esme throws her head back, her face contorting in a silent wail, Esme devolving in his arms.

– Esme, he murmurs into her knotting scalp, her thin hair. – If you let me go and you stay with your granny, later I'll tell you the story about a golden beetle from Jupiter who eats humans. A beetle the size of a man. In a book I'm reading. The scarab injects them with a serum that puts them to sleep, then it eats them up all at once, gulp!

Esme's head stops its automaton rubbing.

She clasps his cheeks with her small, clammy hands and raises her eyes to his mouth, reading his lips for a lie. Her visage ancient.

– Why would a beetle do that, she asks. – Fingernails and elbows too?

– Fingernails and elbows and faces and earlobes. If you go to Granny now, I'll tell you later on, he says.

She abruptly reaches both arms out to Granny. Granny clamps her lips in what he guesses is pleasure and gathers up the little girl.

Flinging along metal tracks in his luxurious prison, somewhere between Medicine Hat and Calgary, Baxter thinks about Edwin Drew.

Mr. Drew in his finely cleaned and pressed monkey suit sailing around like a King of England with his precise pronunciation, his brain a full set of *Encyclopaedia Britannica*, as he showed the new porters all stuffed into the off-duty car how to make down and make up a berth, how to fold a blanket *exactly* by drawing the blanket from the foot to the head, how to shake the curtain to quietly wake up a passenger who has to detrain in the night, how to use the whisk broom on a male passenger's jacket, an ostrich feather duster for cobwebs, how to sponge then dry off a washstand without leaving smears or blots or cloudy patches, the code names for mice (diamonds) and rats (sapphires) and roaches (rubies) and bedbugs (pearls) in a car, how to deal with ladies having lady issues, how to deal with men having men issues, how to deal with drunk passengers (*Make them drunker*, declared Mr. Drew, and he winked at Baxter while all the student porters laughed), how to deal with passengers who'd had too much to drink the night before, how to deal with a disorderly woman or sporting girl plying her wares on the train, how to calm down the sleeptalkers, the sleepwalkers, how to know the time it takes for a train to travel from Chicago to Smiths Falls, or from Duluth to Sault Ste. Marie. The infinite number of protocol crimes that could earn demerits (*disloyalty, dishonesty, the use of intoxicating liquors or frequenting of places where they are sold, immorality, insubordination, incompetence, gross carelessness, untruthfulness*). The infinite crimes that could earn dismissal (*disloyalty, dishonesty, the use of intoxicating liquors or frequenting of places where they are sold, immorality, insubordination, incompetence, gross carelessness, untruthfulness*), how to look in the little instruction handbook with its cardboard covers they all have to carry if they have any questions about the rules. Mr. Drew had a wide, clear face, sported wide shoulders, and Baxter wondered if he engaged in calisthenics.

But when Baxter took a turn to show how he knew how to make up a berth, he had to shove the lower mattress into the upper berth and shove the berth back into place with all his might, sweat pouring down the sides of his head, his eyeglasses sliding down his nose, skating down the nervous moisture. He suddenly understood why Mr. Drew's shoulders and arms wielded so much power, how he swirled and folded sheets like a bullfighter, and snapped up and snapped down the ponderous, heavy berths from the ceiling as though they were made of cloud.

He will not think about his parents back home. He hasn't written a letter in months. Maybe even a year. He smooths out his upper lip as he chews a cold perogy. His mother praying over him, the times she slapped his face because he twirled one too many times in front of his female cousins. He was the best twirler of all of them, the best somersaulter of all of them.

– You're her only son, said his father.

Baxter likes the cold of Canada. Even though he was born in the tropics, he droops in the island's tropical heat. The island hemmed in by ocean he could walk to on all sides if he had time enough, the island hemmed in by aunts and uncles and cousins, and friends of cousins and aunts and uncles who all knew his mother, knew his father, knew when he woke up, when he went to bed, when he walked down a different street than usual just for a change. All the aunts and uncles and cousins and friends of cousins, aunts, and uncles who liked to remind him about the time his mother's lace-trimmed handkerchief fell out of his pocket at school and they never let him forget it.

He wanted to be Captain Nemo and travel far, far away.

– Nemo? asked Aunt Arimenta.

– Nobody. I don't want anybody to know me.

– Hmm, she said.

– *Mobilis in mobili.*

– Eat your conch.

He misses crunching his teeth into Arimenta's cracked conch.

As he chews his stowed-away supply of congealed perogies, he also misses his mother's black-eyed peas and rice. Curried goat. His mother's souse and Johnnycake. His mother stands over him as he sneaks his dinner, even though she lives so very far away.

– Why do you have to eat with your lip up like that? she asks while he bites another piece of perogy with his teeth.

– Like what?

– Like *that*. Like a woman.

Maybe his jaws moving up and down could smother out her voice. On a table in the back of the house, the thorny lemon tree outside the window, his father scribbles out some sentences for next Sunday's sermon, then tucks his pencil back behind his ear.

Baxter sucks out the inside of the perogy.

– Lord give me faith and patience, says his mother, her hands on her hips. – Stop doing that thing with your mouth!

She pulls out her Bible. – Read to me. Her hands trembling.

– What should I read?

– You choose. Wipe your hands first.

She rocks in her chair as he reads aloud.

– There now, she says, patting her hands on her lap. – There now. Nemo. *Mobilis in mobili.*

At the end of the final day of portering lessons at Union Station in Toronto, the other junior porters walked away along the siding, away from the car, in a bedraggled, hopeful group. Baxter lingered as Edwin Drew packed up his shoeshine kit, bedding. As he expertly folded sheets from an earlier demonstration, Edwin Drew told a story about one time when a passenger asked him to fetch a packet of cigarettes from a station, and before he knew it, the train was pulling away and he wasn't on it. Baxter folded pillow slips.

Edwin Drew laughed lustily as he told the story, his laugh pounding and rich. Baxter tried to laugh too. Just the two of them left in the car as Edwin Drew cleared up.

– Never ran so fast in my life, Edwin Drew said.

He pinched the bridge of his nose as he finished laughing, his teeth perfectly symmetrical, perfectly in order.

Baxter smiled and polished his eyeglasses with a handkerchief. Edwin Drew turned down the light and stood in the vestibule doorway, ready to leave. Baxter followed, but stopped short just behind Edwin Drew because Edwin Drew wasn't exiting the car.

– Do you want to have a little fun? whispered Edwin Drew. He brushed a speck of something off Baxter's shoulder.

– Like what? asked Baxter.

Edwin Drew tugged at Baxter's lapels as though to straighten them, then kissed him. Baxter's very first kiss. The kiss astonished him, like he'd been pushed off a cliff and discovered he could fly.

Edwin Drew broke down a berth faster than Baxter had seen in all those two weeks.

Baxter's heart nearly hammered out of his chest at the outrageous perilousness, he thought he might faint at the speed and strength of their tryst, at the wash of joy burning through his every blood vessel as he stroked Edwin Drew's naked chest, his sinewy arms, his skin heated and dark brown like his own, over every bit of skin as they rubbed and sucked each other, hands and mouths and cocks, different keys turning and twisting, fitting, opening. Edwin Drew's perfect, perfect teeth biting Baxter's tongue, spotless tooth enamel grazing his cock.

The inexplicable release he found that night inside that train car, Edwin Drew's toothprints imprinted on his own tongue forever.

Afterward, Baxter stroked the cuff of Edwin Drew's shirt, wanting to crawl inside it and never leave. Baxter tried to kiss Edwin Drew again, the tip of his tongue skipping along the blades of Edwin Drew's teeth. Edwin Drew pushed him away, buttoned his trousers closed, refitted his cap on his head, and told Baxter without words, in the weighted silence of the lower berth in a car on a siding, in their dangerous liaison, that he'd best be on his way.

Baxter lurched out onto the siding tracks. Back onto the street in front of the station, a different man entirely, an addicted man.

Not so far behind him, Edwin Drew whistled a song as he closed up the car, 'The Merry Widow Waltz.'

DAY FOUR

(CALGARY TO BANFF)

– First call for breakfast, sings Kuzyk.

Punch and Judy block Baxter in the passageway, Judy with her fingernail-sized doll's teeth perfect for chomping, Punch with his lips so tight his teeth remain a mystery.

– Will the train be on time? asks Judy. – I don't know how much more I can take of sleeping in the icebox that is our room.

– So much depends upon me not being late, says Punch, his pocket watch open like a halved hardboiled egg in his hand.

Baxter wills his eyes not to roll; he wills so hard his eyeballs crack in the back.

He extracts the timetable from his pocket. Points at the name of a village on the table where the train won't stop because this is the fastest train across the continent.

The Spider and the Tuppers eat calf livers and kidneys at the first sitting, Miss Tupper excited that *Today we'll be in Banff!* Her mother silent with her nose in her romance book, as though in prayer, even as she walks to and from the diner.

– Gooooood morning, Porter! says Dr. Hubble, saluting Baxter so hard he staggers forward. Baxter lunges to help him, but Dr. Hubble has bounced up almost immediately, his face red. He salutes Baxter again and barrels away, whistling the first notes of a nonsense song, no doubt easy because of the way his right incisor slightly overlaps the left, and he pivots off to his breakfast. Baxter sweeps the sheets out of the berths and heaves the mattresses, still warm, up into the ceiling. Even though he asked her politely to make sure she'd gathered up all her things, he finds a wilted nightdress in Miss Tupper's upper berth. Baxter stuffs two items of Miss Tupper's still skin-temperature underthings – she must leave them out on purpose – into a paper bag and heaves them into her upper berth before he shuts it up into the ceiling.

He hovers outside the door to Compartment A, the compartment of the blond man, blond Blancmange and his green-shoed lady friend stowed away, the bell mute as a fish, the arrow on the call board unperturbed.

Baxter dreads the hurricane gathering in that room.

The Spider, her forehead compressed into eight wrinkle lines, pokes at her embroidery, her barrette sparkling. Esme stares at the Spider's barrette.

– What a beautiful view, says the Spider to Granny. – This is a beautiful view, isn't it? The sky so blue and wide.

– Yes.

– Was your daughter at peace when she died?

Granny claps her hands to Esme's ears.

– Yes! says Granny.

– I can help her be at peace. Would that help you? I can help you rest. Help the little girl rest.

– She *is* at peace.

Judy ploofs down beside the Spider. Granny flinches backwards toward the window, her arms crossed, Spider crouches over her embroidery, and the old man with the Napoleon-disguised *Lady Audley* novel sitting across from the Spider huffs to standing and bids them adieu.

The train pulls into Calgary, the sky bright, and outside, one passenger Baxter doesn't recognize and who never slept in his berth once tips him fifty cents as he steps down out of the car. Eighty-two cents total. $94.53 to go.

As Baxter collects his step box and legs it back up into the train, a scream echoes down the platform. He can't tell if it's the train or himself. After five minutes, the train zooms away from this scorched prairie town. He wipes his face with his handkerchief, but the sweat keeps oozing: there are still washstands and floors to wipe after the chaos of the morning, dirty linen from the sleepyheads to roll away in bags in the linen locker. The newlywed couple in Section 4, Mr. and Mrs. Lewington, still have not broken out of their curtained cocoon today, even though he has shaken the curtain several times, cleared his throat several times, and according to his increasingly crumpled list they're supposed to detrain in Banff.

Compartment A's door remains closed and unanswered.

– Maybe this man flew away on a rocket to Mars, says Esme, holding on to his trousers.

– Maybe, he answers.

He counts the towels for the fifty-fifth time. He answers passenger questions about the size of farms, the weight of a grain elevator empty or full, what kind of flowers were those yellow ones with the brown centres that already sped by. He fetches drinks, tells Punch and Judy a joke about how the prairies are so flat, you can watch your dog get lost for days. A joke that is old for him but new for them, and they laugh, Judy's hands over her mouth, Punch holding his hands over his belly he laughs so hard. Punch's back molars studded black in his mouth as he laughs.

assengers bustle off to the second breakfast sitting, and Baxter rushes to their sections, Esme hanging off his back or paddling around at his feet. He folds and clunks and clicks and locks beds away into the ceiling.

The train rumbles too slowly. The pine trees and mountain slopes saunter rather than speed by. He could walk faster than this car's speed right now.

Only one more night to go, and then he can lie down, full-length, on a mattress and fling himself into sleep. His bell rings. Section 4. Finally! He hustles to Section 4.

– Can I help you, shir?

He slurred his words. Did he just say *shir*?

– Have you ever been married? asks the newlywed Mr. Lewington in Section 4, finally out of bed, his pointy-faced Mrs. Lewington sitting beside him. Their honeymoon has already deflated their marriage.

– No, sir, Baxter says.

He can't figure out what the husband wants. Baxter sways, he works every muscle in his body not to fall to the ground.

– Greatest day of a man's life, the husband says, his voice flat.

He reaches across to clasp his wife's hand, but she flicks his hand away. He stands up, pulls his trousers up higher around his waist, and sways back and forth as he picks his way past the other sections to the back end of the train. The wife stands up, shakes out her skirt and picks her way down the aisle in the direction of the front of the train.

The Spider picks at her panel with her needle, shaping out another series of unidentifiable tangles and snags. Maybe a seaside scene? A peacock?

Baxter shrinks back up the aisle backwards, slowly.

Sleepiness drips off him, pools around his feet, forms quicksand that tangles up his feet every now and then, makes him see spots where there are none.

He steps among the passengers in their sections in his white summer jacket, the regulation razor's edge of his ironed trousers starting to blur. Boisterous laughing and talking belches from the smoker, but the smokers cease speaking when he pokes his head in. He nods to the silent men as they sit sprawled around the compartment. Punch smoking a pipe, the young husband, Pulp of Pulp and Paper, smoking. The room redolent with expensive cigar and pipe smoke and flannelmouths.

One day he might be this well-to-do too, smoking and sprawling his way across the continent. Tossing around the dollars, bills crumpled up like spare change in every pocket. Invent and patent a prosthetic-teeth device that will be as important to modern dentistry as pliers.

He travels the length of the car to the women's washroom.

The washroom immaculate except for the shivering man in the middle of the floor, curled into a snail.

He jumps, aware of a person suddenly swooped in close beside him.

– I see him too, says the Spider.

– Yes, madam, he says, because he must be dreaming.

The man shimmers.

The Spider turns and strolls away, her hands clasped behind her back.

Baxter yawns.

The folded postcard has cooled against his chest. So close to his skin, he almost forgets he has it. He should throw it down the hopper.

Baxter rubs a rag over the dust that seems to *grow* from the walls, goddamnit. Esme has returned to his other arm and hangs off his elbow. They toddle by Blancmange's silent Compartment A.

Mad Mary, prowling the car, greets Esme. – Hello, little miss! he pronounces.

He leans to Baxter's ear and says out of the corner of his mouth, – Clean up the ash spilled on the carpet outside the smoker.

He leans in closer and whispers, – You're as useless as a pheasant with phlebitis.

– Goodbye, little miss, he says, loudly, and pats Esme's head. – Toodle-oo!

Baxter hoists Esme up onto his hip. Miss Tupper, her hatboxes gathered up around her, her bags ready, removes the hat on her head and pops on another one, pressing down the crown, fluffing the flower trim, trying to figure out the very best, most flattering hat.

She looks up to Esme planted on Baxter's hip. – Little girl, she says to Esme, – which one looks better, little girl?

– Ehhh, says Esme, – the black one, she says, and she sticks an index finger into her mouth.

– But there isn't a black one.

– Esme, come here, says Granny.

Esme wraps her knees tighter around his waist as she hangs off Baxter. Then she drops to the ground, one bony limb at a time.

Old Napoleon-Lady-Audley takes Esme in his arms and hurls her up into the air like dough for a pizza pie before lumbering off for elsewhere; Pulp and Paper in Section 1 pat her on the crown, then continue fluttering papers and pamphlets back and forth over her head. Mrs. Tupper, readying herself to detrain in Banff, bars Esme with her arm to stop her from stepping on the books stacked and scattered on the floor of her section. – My daughter Carlotta sucked my bosom dry years ago, she says to no one, and then she laughs.

Carlotta, a silky hat the colour of sand settled on her head, flips through a magazine. Napoleon-Lady-Audley turns a page in his book.

The Spider nods at nothing, hearing and seeing something else entirely mid-stitch while her needle and its taut string of embroidery silk stay suspended in the air.

Esme turns into the Spider's section, her eyes fixed on the glittering spider barrette, her tiny hands clenched. She hunches low like a goblin and stares at the Spider. The Spider snaps awake. – Maybe I'll go for a stroll. Would anyone like to join me?

The car rumbles slowly over the tracks. Miss Tupper raises her magazine up closer to her face. Granny looks at her own reflection in the window, a sea of pine forest outside, and Mrs. Tupper restacks three books, first alphabetically, then biggest to smallest.

The Spider draws up her embroidery hoop and blocks her view of Esme. The needle resumes its poking through the linen panel.

Baxter holds his tired hand out to Esme, and they pace the aisle and passageway. Even his knuckles are weary.

The door to the Drawing Room opens, and a gush of cold draft sweeps by him. Judy asks him for a vial of Medicinal Petroleum Oil and a spoon. She has wrapped herself in multiple shawls.

– It's my husband, she says, leaning close to him, her teeth puppet-small.

Baxter grabs Esme up and onto his shoulders and dashes to find Petroleum Oil for Judy.

The woman's wail rattles his eardrums before he has even returned to his car, bottle of Petroleum Oil in hand. Esme's hands clamp on to his temples. He hands off the bottle and spoon to Punch in the doorway of the Drawing Room. Punch grabs them, then slams the door shut.

Miss Tupper holds both her hands to her face, her face swathed in handkerchief, keening and sobbing, her face red and swollen, her hat gone, her hair tangled and dripping around her face. The other women crowd around her. The Spider, her embroidery hoop held up against her chest, murmurs with Judy who's planted herself firmly in the seat opposite Miss Tupper. Mrs. Tupper sits off to the side, her forehead pressed into her tented fingers. Esme's grandmother sits in her own seat, twisting the rings on her fingers round and round. Other passengers in the car, Mr. and Mrs. Lewington, Napoleon-Lady-Audley, mumble among themselves. Most of them scatter away, abandoning their magazine and handkerchief detritus on the seats in their haste, bumping into Baxter as they gallop for the different ends of the car, except for Pulp and Paper who leaf through their papers on the little table between them, crossing and uncrossing their legs. Paper peeks down the aisle only once, then buries his face back in his papers.

– Oh my gosh, says Judy. – Oh my goodness!

– I told you so, says Mrs. Tupper, rubbing her forehead. – A rotten egg.

– Rotten eggs swarm to me! says Miss Tupper. She rocks back and forth.

– Rotten through and through.

– Oh my dear, says Judy.

– Is there anything I can do, miss? asks Baxter. He glances at her mother.

– Esme, says Granny. – Come to me.

She holds her hands up to Esme.

Esme clamps her hands on to Baxter's forehead.

– *Esme*, Granny's voice so low it's almost a growl.

– Miss? says Baxter to Miss Tupper. – Would you like a cup of water?

A scatter of freckles stands out against her face pale as paper. Perhaps he should unearth the smelling salts too.

– That *Gerald*, says Mrs. Tupper, dashing her hands away from her forehead. – We have wasted all this time travelling to *Banff*, to some ridiculous *village* in the *woods*, for no reason at all. The selfish –

She pats her neck with a handkerchief, fans the handkerchief in her face.

– Why did he do it? asks Judy. – Is he a dope fiend?

– The telegram doesn't say, says Miss Tupper.

Mrs. Tupper strangles the handkerchief in her hands.

– I don't understand it, says Miss Tupper. – I've been jilted by telegram? *Telegram*?

– And he wrote me a letter. I wanted to tell you what was in the letter, Carlotta.

– We're done! proclaims Pulp from his section.

– No, we're not, says Paper.

– We're done this chart. I need to smoke, says Pulp. He jumps to his feet and jogs away, his elbows clamped to his sides.

– Oh for the love of –, says Paper. He clenches his jaws and lifts a fist toward Pulp's disappearing back.

Paper violently shuffles papers for a moment, thumps a ledger down on his little section table, then leans out of his and Pulp's section, gripping the upholstery, and peers down the aisle at the cluster of women and Baxter as though uncertain whether he should chase Pulp down in the smoker or somehow come to the aid of the weeping Miss Tupper.

Miss Tupper sobs, and while digging for a handkerchief in her bag, swipes mucus leaking from her nose with the side of her hand. Paper bounds up the aisle and offers her his handkerchief. She grabs it without looking up and crumples it against her eyes. None of the women look up.

Paper hovers, then backs away toward the exit.

– To be frank? says the Spider, – I blame the Banff Springs Hotel. Does anyone want to know why I blame the hotel? I learned about it at my conference in Winnipeg. There was a bride, a heavenly girl, who fell while walking up a set of stairs on her wedding day. She was about to see her groom! Broke her neck. Dead as a doornail in her beautiful wedding dress, her flowers scattered all around her. I am sure your fiancé saw her, perhaps she appeared to him in the night, and he immediately changed his mind.

– Oh, please *stop*, says Mrs. Tupper.

– Or maybe he just got nervous, says the Spider.

Esme's breaths rasp in his ear.

– Oh Porter! says Judy. – Perhaps the young lady might like a glass of water.

– Of course, madam, Baxter says. He lifts his upper lip, shows all his teeth so that she'll like him in spite of her cold room. Ten demerits to go, and he knows Judy will likely be the one who sinks him. He can smell it.

– What a lovely smile you have, she says. – And you would be such a pretty little poppet if you smiled too, says Judy to Esme, who has fitted her chin to the top of Baxter's head.

Esme tightens her claws around Baxter's collarbones.

Baxter draws a glass of water in the smoker while Pulp and Paper smoke cigarettes.

– I didn't say that, says Pulp, stabbing in the air with his index finger. – I would never use that word. George, did I say that?

He coughs in the direction of Baxter and Esme. His cigar breath so acute it burns.

– I must have been out of earshot, sir, says Baxter.

If only the water would pour just a little faster.

– I heard you say it, says Paper.

– Who's George? asks Esme, and Pulp laughs through his nose at her.

– My name's not George, Baxter stutters.

In his head. Only ten demerits to go.

Click click clickety click.

Mountains loom and hem them in on all sides as they trundle toward Banff, tucked among the snowy, stony peaks.

Punch delightedly tells Baxter that they are at least two minutes early because the train didn't stop in Calgary as long as it should have, his pocket watch and chain shining in the palm of his hand.

– The fastest train across the continent, yes sir, Baxter says, his tongue at least thirteen pounds.

He yawns without moving his mouth, without moving a single muscle in his jaws. The inside of his head crumples.

– But it would be terrible if I missed my sister in Sicamous. She would be devastated. Will the train slow down to make up the time?

The train has already slowed down. But only Baxter seems to have noticed. The soles of his feet read that the rumbling along the tracks is not as swift as before.

– Where are we now exactly? asks Punch.

Baxter points vaguely at *Canmore* on the timetable, but it's a place the train won't stop or didn't stop because this is the fastest train across the continent, and Canmore's nothing but a mining town.

Punch wheezes out an asthmatic whistle and walks away jaunty.

Baxter sits on his stool in the smoker, his hands on his knees. Esme hanging off his neck, Rocky curled in her other arm, her lips right next to his ear whispering a story that sounds only like, *sss ssss sss curly bears sss sss baby bassoon ssss*, a story that pokes his brain awake with every *ssss* and stops his head from nodding, his eyelids from flipping out a *Sorry We Are Closed* sign.

The train slows, wheezes. Stops. He imagines it must be for a silk train. Or animals who've meandered on the tracks. The train restarts, lurching, the car's wheels turn again. Ever so slowly. Punch bursts into the smoker. – What's going on? he asks. – What's the delay?

– I'm not sure, sir. Perhaps a silk train coming through.

– Well, find out, says Punch.

– Yes, sir! I'll ask the conductor if he knows.

Punch can go suck an egg. Baxter lurches up to standing.

Mrs. Tupper and Judy huddle together with the Spider in the Spider's section. Mrs. Tupper shakes her head as Judy babbles a low monologue, and the Spider punctures and repunctures her embroidery panel with her needle without looking down. Judy fans her face with a lacy Spanish fan, too hot in this section, too cold in her Drawing Room, her earrings tinkling and sparkling, and they all erupt in subdued laughing. Carlotta Tupper huddles in the corner of her section by the window.

Baxter sits on his stool in the smoker, a hand placed on each knee, Esme and Rocky on the floor at his feet. Under the bench in front of him, the curled man trembles, but he has turned over, his spine facing out, the dusty soles of his black-socked feet bony and long.

When Aunt Arimenta was sick, she lay curled up too, her back to him. He moved around the bed to the other side so he could see her face. But her eyelids were pressed closed.

– Don't go, he said.

– Everyone has to go, she said. – Hold my hand.

He stroked her bulbous, wrinkled knuckles, the veins along the backs of her hands. He couldn't save her life, no matter how much he wept.

– You're a special boy, she said.

She had saved $362 from decades of selling eggs and sewing and not feeding herself enough. And she gave it all to him.

So he could be Nemo.

So he rode a boat away from the island and toward university in North America, her death the final push out the door, enough money in his pocket for the country to let him in.

He yawns, and the curled man flips face out. Baxter jerks up to standing, and Esme climbs his leg. He catches her up in his arms. He walks away from the curled man as quickly as he can.

The Spider stitches a last stitch, knots her last knot in her monstrous embroidered scene. She unsnaps her embroidery panel from the hoop, and the other women coo over it, tracing the lines with their fingertips. The stitched surface bristles with snarls, crooked and patchy blobs, and she gently lays it in her small bags. She unfolds a new piece of fabric, snaps it into the hoop, threads new silk into her needle, and pokes a first stitch into a new scene. A cushion cover.

– What will this one be? asks Judy.

– A radish dancing with a scallion.

– Lovely, says Judy.

Baxter paces to the other end of the car, then back again, Esme and Rocky in his arms. The quivering man has writhed his way into the men's washroom, has coiled himself up under the line of washbasins. Baxter takes a deep breath and leans down to better see the quivering man's face, but the man shakes so hard his features blur and all Baxter can see are the bared teeth. Baxter stands up again and looks out the window at an army of pine trees crawling up the side of a mountain.

– What were you looking at? asks Esme, both arms around her horse.

P ine trees and jagged rock gloom on both sides as the car trundles slower and slower, the train crawling as it twists and switches its way through forest and rock. One time a human foot surfaces in the rock, all five toes, a heel. Baxter rubs his eyes with both fists.

Miss Tupper asks what time they'll be in Banff. Her nose and eyes stained red from weeping.

– According to the schedule, says Miss Tupper, a wrinkle etched between her eyebrows, – we should have arrived in Banff twenty minutes ago. I just want to get off this train. I want to go home.

– Sometimes delays happen along the way, even on the fastest train across the continent, Baxter says, – but it's always about placing passenger safety and comfort first. Perhaps you might try the solarium. The view of the mountains is quite lovely indeed, and the solarium is one of the finest features of this train.

He staggers. Just a small stagger. Esme wails when Granny pulls her away by the arm to come eat lunch.

Sleep has a smell. He can tell he's just had a tiny nap during that page flip in Mrs. Tupper's book because of the fleeting wisp of smell deep behind his nose.

He pivots because just now he's heard the echo of his bell, and he can't wait to see what tiny but huge theatrics must be summoning him to one of the compartments, perhaps even Compartment A.

Sleep has a taste. He can tell he's had an accidental sip because of its thick flavour crouched far back in his mouth where the root of his tongue meets the deep hook of his throat.

As he trots down the narrow aisle between the sections, outside the window a naked man climbs like a squirrel up the trunk of a tall, spindly pine tree.

After acres of aching slowness, the train wheezes onto a siding and stops.

– Why aren't we moving? asks Punch, the chain of his pocket watch clinking in his fingers.

Out the left-hand side window, sliced rock face peers back at them. The right-hand side, a mountain meadow on the edge of a vast gorge brimming with mist.

– Are we so high in the mountains we're above the clouds? asks Punch in a very high voice.

– Oh my gracious, says Judy. – Oh my golly.

She holds on to Punch's arm. He pats her hand. – We'll be out of here soon.

Mad Mary barrels down the aisle.

– A mudslide up ahead on the tracks, says Mad Mary. – We'll be on our way again in no time.

– This porter said he asked you why the train stopped and you didn't know. He said that we stopped for a silk train.

Mad Mary tucks his watch into his breast pocket. – Well, sir, this porter here's not so bright.

He starts to laugh.

– Heh heh heh, says Punch.

Baxter expects he's supposed to laugh at himself too, but his lips won't drag open properly.

– That said, says Mad Mary, – sometimes a delay can involve a silk train or a bear or mountain goats on the tracks. It's not an *unreasonable* guess.

– But I must arrive in Sicamous by 7:50 p.m. I *must* speak with my sister.

– Here, says Mad Mary, handing Punch a slip of paper. – A drink, no cost, in the club car to make up for the inconvenience.

– But I was told that this train was supposed to be the fastest train across the continent. That, sir, is clearly a bald-faced lie.

– Oh, it's still the fastest train, sir.

– Hardly, says Punch.

Mad Mary smiles relentlessly, clicks his ticket puncher in his pocket.

Baxter bustles away to the sections. Esme crawls out from Granny's section up the aisle, up his leg, and then clutches on to his thumb.

Miss Tupper, jilted bride in her flowery travelling dress, sits up straight and ready to detrain, her brokenness polished and dusted, a handbag on her lap. As the minutes, then the quarter hours and then one hour, then one hour and a half, ooze by, she sinks more and more into her seat, a springy cake falling and blackening in an oven.

– This is abominable! shouts Punch in his Drawing Room.

His shout settles out, rippling into silence.

They all sit, suspended in the mountains.

Miss Tupper and her mother weren't part of any of the lunch services because they were supposed to detrain at 10:55 a.m.

– I'll get us something to eat, says Mrs. Tupper.

– I don't know, says Miss Tupper.

Mrs. Tupper and Paper pass each other, bumping each other in the aisle. Mrs. Tupper's bottom lip juts out oh so slightly. Paper bites his moustache with his bottom teeth. He pats his pockets as though he's forgotten something and turns around, following her.

– Where are you going? asks Pulp, leaning out of his section.
– Where the devil – ?

Miss Tupper makes no sound except for an occasional clearing of her throat, a squeak of leather as she rubs her shoes together like a cricket. Paper swivels his head at her squeaking feet.

Mad Mary strolls through the aisle and hands every passenger a slip of paper to exchange for a free beverage today in the club car.

Mrs. Tupper returns with a wax-paper package, places it on the bench beside her, opens her book, chews her thumb, and starts to read.

– I'm not hungry, says Miss Tupper.

Mrs. Tupper turns a page. Nudges off the heel of one of her shoes and lets the shoe dangle from her stockinged toes.

Miss Tupper's right hand darts out and she unwraps the wax paper from the sandwich. She bites off a tip, folds the paper back around the bread and meat, and places it beside her mother's hip.

Baxter's mouth waters.

Paper returns to his section, smoothing down his hair.

The train stands now waiting, hours late. The narrow brim of Miss Tupper's hat wilts. Punch paces and rants in his room, leaning on the bell for updates. Judy strolls with the Spider through the cars, whispering about matters spiritual and minding other passengers' business. They are on the hunt for the famous actor they heard about in the dining car. Passengers swarm Mad Mary, wanting to know if they can get off the train and go for a walk even though there's no platform, even though the locomotive could start again at any moment. Against the rules. Against the rules! Plus, they've been soiling the tracks underneath the cars these past few hours. The tracks, the underside of the train, are now one long, luxurious latrine, Baxter is sure.

Baxter creeps toward the ghostly silent Compartment A.

He balances a clean towel draped over one arm, a water jug frosty with condensation in the other. Baxter presses the bell.

He hears the thump and bump of boxes, footsteps.

The door opens a crack. A blond, Blancmange eyeball squints at Baxter, then the door cracks open further. The man scuttles back to one of the seats.

– Please shut the door behind you, he says. – I don't want strangers to know I'm here.

Oh God, he's probably ill. Where's the woman?

Blancmange flops onto his back on one of the sofas, a book in his hands, his eyebrows and eyelashes sparkling. His feet in white-and-black wingtip dancing shoes on the upholstery.

Shoes on the seat, a woman stowed away in secret, the garbage can stuffed and spilling with crumpled papers, wrappers, orange peels, two china plates, and soiled cloth napkins from the diner! Baxter sets the jug down next to the commode.

– Fresh towels for you, sir. Anything I can get you, sir? You rang. I'll empty that trash can right away.

– No. I did not ring, Blancmange says, turning a page in his book. – I'm fine. Go away. Please shut the door all the way, I don't want anyone to know I'm here.

Baxter sways. Blinks away the sleepiness clawing into his scalp.

He does not want to have to clean up vomit if this man decides to be sick. The smell of vomit will make him vomit. He steps into the compartment and replaces a wrinkled, moist towel; wipes water droplets off the basin.

– Lunch will be served soon in the diner if you'd like to eat out there with the other passengers.

– I really just want to lie here and read my book.

– All right, Baxter says, shutting the door behind him. He forgot to say *sir*.

– *Sir*, he sneers, under his breath.

He trips on a bump of air because he fell asleep momentarily. He checks in on the sections.

Too many hours have passed, and the passengers' restlessness slimes down the aisles, sags against the windows, their swelling impatience a wraith twisting and whining among the sections and passageways. Baxter's bell rings. Dr. Hubble from Compartment B paces the passageway up and down, over and over again, and even though Baxter says to him, *Come ahead, come ahead*, the Doctor refuses to come ahead, – I'm exercising, he says. – You come ahead, Porter, and both he and Baxter flatten sideways, their fronts facing, their chests grazing, as Baxter passes, flustered and apologizing as he rushes to his call board. The tiny metal arrow on his call board points again at Goddamn Punch and Goddamn Judy in the Goddamn Drawing Room.

Punch opens the door, hopping in irritation, wanting to know, demanding to know. The Spider's planted herself inside their room and wrapped herself up in a blanket, enthralled in conversation with Judy who's bundled herself up in a cocoon of shawls.

Punch flumps down into his seat in irritation. Baxter has almost closed the door when Judy stands up and speaks.

– Porter, calls Judy, – I have been aboard this train since Montreal.

He already knows this. Does Judy think he doesn't know this? Does she think he hasn't noticed the constant nattering? Baxter quietly cracks a knuckle. He tries to keep from swaying because it's not acceptable to sway unless the train is moving. She might complain and he'll get written up. She glides toward him, her jewelled fingers clutching her shawls around her.

– And, she continues, – this compartment is haunted. Mrs. Crane can confirm this.

– Yes, without a doubt, says the Spider. – I feel a very queer, almost *electrical* energy in here. Hence the temperature irregularity. Isn't that right, Judith?

– And my husband's and my disturbed sleep, Judy says. – Our digestive upsets.

– I have eaten identical items, says the Spider, – *identical*, and experienced no upset.

Bored. What Judy knows about disturbed sleep won't fill a thimble. And now the Spider has extruded her silk and is hauling Judy in.

Baxter steeples his fingers.

He half steps into the lavish room, Punch and Judy recoiling, the Spider bolted to her seat, so many bodies staining this room, and he quickly scans the ceiling and panelled walls because that is what they seem to want him to do, as though he could just sweep away any phantasm with an ostrich feather duster, like a long, looping cobweb draped over the washstand.

Baxter feels another yawn welling up from his deepest gut. It ripples out, dissipates as soon as it reaches his jaws because he cannot yawn in front of them. The last time he yawned in a passenger's face, his jaws craned apart of their own volition, and he thought the passenger hadn't noticed until he detrained in Toronto and that passenger had written a letter to the superintendent. Back at headquarters Baxter got punched in the guts with twenty demerits for disrespect.

– I'm doubling the demerits because this is the second time. And that's me being a good Christian, the superintendent said from behind his desk, not even looking at Baxter, instead leafing through the papers in front of him while he scrubbed out pencilled words here and there with a grimy eraser, the tip of his gummy tongue sticking out from the exertion. – That passenger wanted you fired for insubordination, he said. – I'm doing you a favour, don't you forget it.

Punch pops up. – Now, Judith, he says, – I have it all under control.

– I have been trying to disregard it, husband, she says to Punch, – but I cannot any longer.

Judy gestures widely, the lace edging of one of her sleeves thwacking Baxter. She leans toward Punch. – The jig. Is. Up, she says.

Punch puffs out his lips as he sighs, his head silhouetted by a close of pine trees outside the window. One of the pine trees ejects a puff of vapour.

– Our dilemma is not ghosts, says Punch. – Our dilemma is not making it to Sicamous within the proper twenty-four-hour period. This is unacceptable, Porter. Simply outrageous.

What does Punch expect him to do, what does Judy want him to do? The compartment flickers, an empty shell.

– I would like to hold a séance in our compartment tonight, says Judy. – I require a small table. Candles.

A bump from Compartment A reverberates through the wall.

Baxter stifles a shout, and he curls his toes.

– Of course, madam, he says. – How many candles will you require?

She leans toward him, the walls forcing them in so close he can see the pores in her daughter-of-abolitionists nose.

– Thirty-nine exactly.

– Three goes into thirty-nine thirteen times, says Punch. – That's a good number. Certainly superior to forty-two.

Baxter will tell her he can spare only two candles. All right, three candles, because clearly three holds a special value with this couple of cuckoos. Mad Mary will understand the fire risk of thirty-nine blazing candles in a *Drawing Room* under the supervision of Judy Gone Balmy. So would a spotter. *Anyone* would understand.

– We will have a séance with thirty-nine candles. We will discover who is disturbing our sleep in this room –

– May I interrupt, says the Spider. – One candle will do. Too much light, and the spirit controls may be stingy with their visitation.

He scratches the back of his neck, behind one of his ears, the tickling behind his ears, worried about how long his hair's gotten. Is getting, as this trip lengthens. He should have gone to the barber in Montreal. But that barber and his tawdry hijinks. One of these people could be a spotter out to get him. This request must be a test. Ten more demerits. Thirty-nine candles. His hair has grown an inch every time he catches his reflection.

Why didn't he get his hair cut before this run? He'll lose his job. Because of that barber in Montreal.

– What's wrong with you, you don't have a girl? the barber in Montreal asked the last time Baxter sat in his barber's chair, scissors snipping at the back of Baxter's neck, cold whenever they snicked near Baxter's skin. – Smart guy like you. My niece, now she'd make a fine wife. She's smart but not too smart, and shucks, here she is *now*. What a lucky *coincidence!* Hello, Frances! Did you say hello to your mother for me?

Baxter hunched in the barber's chair. Luckily the niece didn't smile once, even as her uncle speechified about how smart and enchanting she was with her piano playing and embroidery talents, how Baxter worked for the railroad so he was a real big shot and looked so smart now with his hair just about trimmed, – Doesn't he look smart, Frances? The answer is yes.

Rolling her eyes behind her glasses, she handed her uncle a wrapped beef sandwich sent by her mother, then stuffed her hands into the pockets of her shapeless grey coat.

– Mother wants to know when you'll be able to cut Vincent's hair, she said.

– Did she remember this time to put enough mustard on the beef? answered the barber.

She softly ground the floor with her heel as her uncle besieged them with his yabber about the fine points of mustard, *how fine and symmetrical Baxter's head is, hey Franny? The brains in this head! Always reading. Just like you.* His scissors exclamation marks as they snipped the hair around Baxter's forehead, the tendons standing out on the back of his neck.

Like the fact that a young, single man like Baxter doesn't have a girl at every station means he has a daisy between his legs instead of a proper cock. He's not a *sailor*. He's not a returned soldier looking for trouble. He just wants to read his books. Those scissors repeatedly slicing and jabbing at his head, held hostage.

Larry, the barber in Vancouver, on the other hand, only ever talked about himself and his blasted, ungrateful children, and when one of his ungrateful sons cut Baxter's hair, the son didn't talk at all, the scissors silver sparks and flashes around Baxter's head, he was so quick, so silent. The Ungrateful Son lay down his scissors and gave a shrug to show he was done cutting and said not a single word.

– One candle will do, repeats the Spider.

Mad Mary confirms it: a mudslide has trapped them in the mountains. They are already almost fourteen hours late.

While Esme waits outside the door, Baxter sits on the toilet briefly, his bowels squeezing out nothing but air, and flips open the folded postcard. These men are not lying with each other in the dark, but in bright sunlight. He tucks it back in his breast pocket.

Back outside, he slips his book out from his locker. Esme traces the scarab imprinted on the cover. – Pretty, she murmurs.

He pulls out the mattress for the seat in the smoker. – Maybe try to sleep, he says to Esme.

Esme lies flat on her back on the sofa, her body stiff and her eyes wide open. He plants himself on a stool at the end of the aisle, the curtained tunnel of sleeping people in their sections snoring ahead of him.

His head nods, then jerks awake. A perfectly ordinary tabby cat swirls around his feet, winding its snaky, muscled tail around his calf, then disappears when he blinks twice. His hand lifts and moves in a circle, wiping out an ashtray hovering in the air before him.

One of the berth curtains swells, then breaks opens before he can even bring over the ladder, and a lady he's never seen before leaps down in a shiny dressing gown, the dressing gown billowing out in butterfly wings. She ignores him as she creeps down the aisle. She tiptoes to another berth two sections down, parts the curtain, and slips inside. She doesn't care what he thinks, none of them do, and whom would he tell? Mad Mary? Laughable. Too bad the lady tiptoes with seagull's feet.

The passengers toss and snore in their berths, loud now without the sound of the train rumbling and rattling over the tracks. The night calm and strange enough for him to contemplate reading his book.

In the dim light, he flips through pages of *The Scarab from Jupiter*. The plucky group of Egyptologists has been abducted to

Jupiter and they sit huddled in a cave in the centre of Scarab City, filled with its pyramids of gold. The man with the scarab in his head is a picked-clean skeleton now, the scarab's larvae having eaten their fill.

Baxter swipes at his leg to knock off the beetle creeping up his trouser leg.

Templeton asks him to watch his car, so Baxter strolls the passageway in Templeton's car to stay awake, Esme holding his hand, carefully stepping each foot ahead of the other as though on a tightrope. Templeton's car is all sleeping compartments, no sections, no Drawing Room. Baxter's shoulders graze the shining walls and doors, and he stands at the door leading to the vestibule. He picks away at his reflection in the window, holes where his eyes should be. He backs up and unlocks the door to this car's linen locker. Baxter closes the door. Why did he open it in the first place?

Mrs. Tupper backs out the door of one of the compartments, tousled and fastening the front of her kimona. She is half-smiling, her teeth tiny lights in the half dark, until she turns and sees Baxter. She freezes, like an actress in a motion picture, her mouth an O. Then she swishes down the corridor, her smile back on, her smell musky. Baxter stuffs himself into the corner, a conch darting into its shell.

– Good evening, madam, Baxter whispers.

She turns back, holds out a dollar. Oh, he's dreaming. No he's not: $93.53 to go.

She holds her fingertip to her lips. Shushes him like he is her naughty child.

As the vestibule door closes behind her, the compartment door opens again and Paper emerges, stroking his moustache.

– Shall I fetch the ladder and follow you to your berth, sir? asks Baxter.

– Not yet, says Paper. – I think I'll have a pipe first.

The dollar in his pocket, he strolls back to his own car, to the men's lavatory, Esme swirling around his feet. The bell rings.

Granny.

He and Esme trundle to her section.

– Esme, says Granny. – Esme. Hold my hand. Come try to sleep with Granny.

– Baxter needs me to help him line up his arrows properly, says Esme.

– That kind of work isn't for little girls, says Granny.

– Maybe you can help Granny sleep, Esme, says Baxter.

– I don't need help sleeping! says Granny to Baxter. – Far from it, and frankly I sleep better on my own than with a little girl kicking her feet into my stomach.

Granny needs a good shake.

– Maybe you can read Granny a story.

– Can I read Granny your story? From your book? asks Esme.

His book. She wants his book. He doesn't want to give her his book.

– Certainly, he says.

He memorizes his bookmarked page in case she loses the tattered old bookmark: page 123. 203 pages to go. He hands over his book from his pocket. Esme grabs for it like a squirrel snatching a sunflower seed.

He closes the curtain on Esme and Granny, Esme whispering as she says aloud the words she surely cannot read.

Templeton returns in the dim light. Gives a silent nod to Baxter. Baxter collapses onto his stool. His eyelids slam closed.

The bell clangs his brain awake. He stumbles to his feet. His stomach heaves up into his nose. Compartment B.

Dr. Hubble would like two glasses brought to his compartment, so Baxter hustles to the club car for glasses and sets the tray down on a little table in the compartment.

– Hmm, says the Doctor. – Would you have time to share a drink? he asks.

Baxter shakes his head violently. This is exactly a moment that Edwin Drew described as a classic spotter trap. – I'm sorry, sir, but that's against the rules, he says.

– Oh, says the Doctor. – Of course. Not fair of me to ask.

For someone so important, the Doctor strikes Baxter as a particularly lonely fellow if a porter is the only person he's opting to drink with.

The Doctor sits on the edge of his bed. Wipes under one of his eyes with his thumb. Then the other eye. Then he covers his face with his hands and exhales. His inhale is snotty and full of water.

Baxter has never seen a man cry quite like this outside of a motion picture screen, and that picture was a comedy with the actor only pretending to cry. He is not prepared for the awkward peculiarity of the tears, how the Doctor fights to wipe them away as quickly as they seep from his eyes, as though they are filthy. He hiccups. The tears keep coming. Baxter continues standing, shifting from foot to foot as he witnesses this downpour of sadness.

– Would you like to borrow my handkerchief? asks Baxter.

The Doctor dabs his eyes, returns the handkerchief.

– That's kind of you, he says. He hiccups.

The Doctor reaches into a bag under his berth and tugs out a flask. He tips his wrist up as he sips from the flask.

– You can't drink, but can you sit?

Baxter leans backwards into the chair next to the commode. He rests his palms on his knees, ready to jump, ready to flee.

– My colleague, he hiccups, – my *friend*, David. Well, we were supposed to be travelling together on this trip, but he was arrested. Oh, I guess I should use a glass.

– I'm very sorry to hear that.

– My *good* friend, he repeats, his glass clinking against the tray. – Do you understand what I mean?

He wipes his nose on the edge of his bedsheet.

– I'm sorry to hear about your friend, Baxter says. He curls his fingers around his kneecaps.

The Doctor looks at Baxter with the eyes of a stray mutt, his eyes wet, his nose wet. Baxter thinks about how the sun will surely rise in just an hour. His stomach growls for the one stale perogy left in his locker.

– My aunt Arimenta, says Baxter, carefully, – always used to say, *Baxter*, she'd say, *hearts will never be practical until they can be made unbreakable.*

The Doctor's mouth twitches at the corner.

He nods, then breathes out a small laugh, violently palming the wet corners of his eyes at the same time. The teeth in the top row are all neat and straight in their upper bed of too much gum, the lower teeth also neat and straight. But his lips don't align when his mouth is closed, his mandible is misaligned with his superior maxillary bone. He burrows for a handkerchief in a pile of clothes on the floor by the bed and blows his nose again.

Baxter laughs too even though the Doctor is a white man, a passenger, and no friend, he might even be a spotter masquerading as a passenger, but Baxter knows what a shattered heart feels like, he believes the Doctor about his friend David, the way a broken heart can gash a fellow in the ribs every time he takes a breath.

– Cheers, says the Doctor, and he takes another sip, smiling with his mouth and the corners of his eyes, as though he means it, as though Baxter might offer friendship. Baxter smiles back. Baxter picks up his tray.

– Do you have to go? asks the Doctor.

Baxter pauses. – Would you like me to get you anything else?

– I mean –, says the Doctor. – No.

Baxter shuts the door behind him. The Doctor's face is wide and clear, like Edwin Drew's. He has the gangly limbs of Nicholas Lesiuk. A sweetly crooked mouth.

Baxter punches down the thought.

Morning. A newly birthing sun cracks through the trees and lances straight into his blazing red eyes. Baxter is a sleeping car porter. A sleepy car porter. A sleepy porter he is car. Car sleepy. Porter. Sleeping.

He giggles. Esme folds and unfolds a hand towel into and out of a triangle shape, the edges out then in then out then in. Granny rang early and gave him his book back, handing it to him with the very tips of her fingers as though she was afraid she might actually touch him. He stowed it back in his locker, behind the sleepy-clan man, curled in his glowing ball.

He shovels down a paltry breakfast behind the curtain while a passenger slides a knife into a heaping plate of food on the other side. Didn't he just eat breakfast? The only noise is Templeton's chewing almost drowned out by rhythmic clanking, huffing steam, and wheels and rods turning and grinding over rails. No, that was two days ago. This train stands immobile, surrounded by birds, trees, bears, and evil mountains that seem to grow closer and closer by the hour. He keeps forgetting.

Baxter's thick, sleepy tongue clogs his mouth, and he can tell he ground his teeth in his one-quarter hour of half sleep curled up on the sofa in the smoker because his temporomandibular joint feels as sore as if he chewed and swallowed a new rubber ball.

The chef swigs from a bottle of something. He bugs his eyes out at Baxter, who's been staring. Has he been staring?

The chef waves the bottle in Baxter's direction. – For *halitosis*, he says.

He goes back to slamming egg after egg into a rim of a bowl. Slaps a stack of raw chops onto a metal platter.

Halitosis. Sure.

Baxter wipes his mouth, his stomach still squalling after the tiny portion, and pushes his chair away from the table. Templeton stands up from the table, slaps his own face, once on each side, the crack of each slap a countdown to the beginning of the day.

– Ready, says Templeton.

He pokes his finger into Baxter's shoulder.

– Ha ha! I saw you eyeing those pork chops, he says to Baxter. – One day we'll be home again, then you can eat all the pork chops you want.

– I hope so, says Baxter.

Templeton pokes Baxter in the shoulder again. – Chin up, fella. *Chin up, fella.*

As Baxter slams through vestibule door after vestibule door on his way back from the diner to his car, he passes through the moist air under a pine tree, past the bricks that make up a factory wall in a laneway, past a lavatory stall with a hole in a partition in a Union Station. Arimenta's cracked conch fresh off the stove, a former friend's callused hands, the men twined together on the postcard, and the invisible man who hid the postcard, who continues to torment him with this very cruel prank even though he probably detrained days ago, before this protracted, preposterous delay in the mountains.

The sun only pretends to rise, still just nosing into this day, drawing this day toward its very longest. The sun hates him.

He pauses in the vestibule just prior to his own car, his palm resting on the door. He thinks of the doctor and his friend tumbling into and among those sheets.

How many more hours of this? He pushes through the door. He washes his face, his teeth.

The sun higher, him chasing passengers with the ladder as they erupt through the draperies, drop down and out of their berths.

– I didn't sleep a wink, says Miss Tupper, crookedly buttoning up her cardigan. – Oof, it's chilly this morning.

– Mmm, says Mrs. Tupper, stroking her flattened hair and checking the seam running up the back of her hose as she waits for her daughter to rebutton her cardigan.

– Please don't make us sit with those Pulp and Paper men again, Miss Tupper whispers to her mother. – Feels like the thirteenth time in a row.

She pulls off and puts on her engagement ring, now on her pinky, then the tip of her thumb, rubs the stones against her skirt, polishing, repolishing the emerald face over and over. – The one is too flirty.

– I doubt you'd even know what flirting was if you saw it, yawns her mother. – Oops! I'm sorry. I shouldn't have said that.

– No, you shouldn't have said that, says Miss Tupper.

– Do *not* forget that I am your *mother*.

The Doctor saunters into the smoker while Baxter is in the midst of setting out fresh matches, but when he sees Baxter, he backs up, right out the door, and dashes away in one direction, then back in the other direction, dabbing his forehead.

Baxter counts on his fingers and worries about Blancmange and his stowaway. If he reports Blancmange, Blancmange will complain, and he'll get demerits even though he was doing his job. Five demerits? Ten demerits? Probably two demerits. If he doesn't report Blancmange and Mad Mary finds out about the stowaway lady, he'll get demerits because he wasn't doing his job. Five demerits? Ten demerits? Probably fifteen demerits.

Lurching into the diner, he tramps up to Mad Mary where he sits during the third sitting out among the passengers, a full plate of breakfast laid out in front of him in the half-empty car, the passengers at the other end of the diner. Esme sits on Baxter's shoulders, her tiny fingers twined around his ears, plastered to his forehead.

– Mr. Magruder, he says.

– Hello, missy, says Mad Mary, crinkling his eyes at Esme.

Esme's fingers clench. Mad Mary bites into a slice of fried potato, the fat greasing his chin.

– What, Baxter? asks Mad Mary.

– Got a passenger in a compartment who's locked himself in and won't eat. Doesn't want his berth made up. Haven't seen him eat once in all the days.

– Well ring the bell on the door!

– He told me not to disturb him. He told me to leave him alone.

– I'll come by later.

Mad Mary cuts into his poached eggs. The yolks run creamy over his toast, his perfectly crisped potato, a slice of roasted tomato, and so much saliva collects in Baxter's mouth, he has to swallow three times.

Mad Mary jams his knuckle into the buzzer on the door to Compartment A.

– Sir? he says, firmly. – This is the conductor.

The door stays shut.

Mad Mary plants his ear against the door, the watery old-lady blue of his real eye bright against the bloodshot.

– I'll be back, he says to Baxter, and lumbers off down the passageway.

The compartment door whams open. Baxter jerks backwards, Esme on his shoulders holding on with her knees.

– LEAVE ME ALONE! says Blancmange. – FUCK!

Esme's bony fingers nearly rip off Baxter's ears. He grabs her ankles to stop her from tumbling off.

Blancmange's lips glitter red with paint, and black kohl circles his eyes just like Theda Bara's in *Cleopatra*.

Mr. Blancmange wears a green dress. The colour of new leaves.

A pearl rope so long it drapes down to his stomach and moves up and down on his panting chest. He wears a blond flapper's wig. He is beautiful. He is *beautiful*.

– Oh, whispers Blancmange, grabbing his pearls in a fist. – It's just you. I thought those Dumb Doras from next door had recognized me. Make the conductor go away. Tell him any lie you have to. Also, I'd like a roast beef sandwich. Please.

Blancmange moves to shut the door. Stops.

– Hello, little girl, he says.

The door slams closed.

Please.

Mad Mary soars back down the passageway toward Baxter.

No one ever says *please*. But then Blancmange ruined it by slamming the door in his face. Like Baxter isn't a *person*. With *feelings*.

Punch and Judy poke their heads out of their room.

– What was that shouting? asks Judy. – Has he come out of his room yet?

– Passenger just asking for a roast beef sandwich, says Baxter, smiling blandly. – He's asked me to fetch him a roast beef sandwich.

– Well, says Punch looking to Judy, his nose round and red, – a roast beef sandwich. I could do with a roast beef sandwich. What about you, Judith?

– A roast beef sandwich sounds delicious right now, she says, and claps her hands, her bracelets jingling. – We'll get a roast beef sandwich, just like Andrew Swain!

– Boy, says Punch to Baxter, – fetch two roast beef sandwiches! *Click. Click.*

Esme knocks one of her heels into his chest.

Punch grins wide, proud of providing for himself and his wife, hunter to her spiritualist gatherer.

– Andrew Swain? gasps Mad Mary. – Did you say *Andrew Swain?*

– *Yes. I. Did*, says Judy, clapping her hands with joy. – Andrew Swain is on this train! He's in the compartment next door to *ours!* And Mrs. Crane has determined that our compartment is haunted! This is truly the best holiday I have ever had in my entire life.

Boy. Baxter fixes his eyes on them from under his exhausted eyelids, a sneer he cannot help rising to his face like a kraken from the deep, a tectonic shift of hatred in his chest.

Mad Mary taps him on the shoulder.

– Baxter will happily get you two roast beef sandwiches, says Mad Mary. – Won't you, Baxter.

– Two roast beef sandwiches coming up, yes sir!, he says, his mouth clicking awake like a human's. – Yes, sir!

Mad Mary shushes Punch and Judy, and bustles them back into the Drawing Room.

– I'd like a roast beef sandwich too, calls the Spider from inside the room. Judy and the Spider fling their arms around each other and bob up and down in delight.

Such luck!

– You didn't say it was *Andrew Swain* in Compartment A, whispers Mad Mary. – That explains a lot. He's travelling under a fake name. You better go get that sandwich right away.

Teeth make so much more sense than people. When teeth trouble you, you extract them. Roots hanging, splayed in the clutches of your dental pliers. The rot eradicated. The hole in the gum where the tooth grew, stitched closed. Easy and clean.

Blancmange's teeth showed consistent calculus at the gum line. His mouth, everyone's mouths, protozoa soups. Baxter imagines using pliers on them all. Pull their heads off by the roots.

Blancmange swirls out of his compartment in his silk and pearls and knocks on the door to the Drawing Room.

Judy opens the door and squeals.

– Did one of you say this room was haunted? asks Blancmange. – Are you Sarah Crane, the famous medium? Do you conduct private séances? I need to do a private séance with you.

– Please *do* come *in*, Mr. Swain, says Judy, her rosy cheeks the rosiest they've ever been.

Mad Mary announces that they will release the passengers into the wild.

– Please exit only through the car Renfrew or the rear solarium car. Ladies and gentlemen, please stay away from the edge of the gorge.

Baxter opens the trap door and pokes his head out of the vestibule. A breeze puffs up into the hole and into the sweating train. The sun blares from above, groves of lodgepole pines and covens of poplars dot along the track. Craggy lower mountains blanketed in trees, higher mountaintops traced with capillaries of snow loom around them. Intersecting the tracks, a faint dirt road. A road leaping off into the gorge as the train stands in the centre of a faded, demented crossroad.

– Well, *this* is no good, says Baxter.

– Why? asks Esme.

– Aunt Arimenta always said it was bad luck to linger at a crossroad.

Esme grips his thumb, presses the edge of one of her nails into the fleshy part.

Baxter steps down and outside, the fresh mountain air rushing and smelling of pine trees and bitter sap. He helps passengers step and crunch down onto that strange, faded road while Esme stands beside him, one hand hanging on to his pant leg.

Mad Mary and the porters from the other cars catch and release passengers as they descend from the train, through car Renfrew, and out the solarium car. Baxter, Ferdinand, Templeton, Freckles, and A.P. cup elbows and clutch hands as they ease passengers out of the train, hover their hands in front of other passengers as they jump down. Mad Mary chats with the passengers about the view, opening his arms wide to the forest as though he made the trees himself, looking especially avuncular and proud as he follows through on this dodo decision, strolls among them with his too-loud joviality as he shatters Instruction Manual railway rules into smithereens. What if someone gets eaten by a bear? Back in the car, Baxter tucks Esme behind him, her hands hugging his knees as the passengers flood down the passageways and spurt and jostle out the doors, exclaiming at the mountains, the air so chill and fresh it makes them cough, the gorge bubbling with fog. One of them drops what must be half a box of crackers in his car as the crowd stampedes for the door. The rest of the passengers crumble and trample the crackers into the carpet, but Baxter continues smiling, tamping down a gush of irritation. Pulp sneezes, then snuffles into a giant handkerchief, working it with his finger up into the wide wells of his nostrils as he dips out of the train. Paper stays in the car and continues working on his papers at the little table in their section.

Out the open vestibule door, standing on a fallen log carpeted with moss, Mad Mary makes a pronouncement: – Ladies and gentlemen, PLEASE STAY AWAY FROM THE EDGE OF THE GORGE.

Pulp gallops up to the edge of the gorge, stretches his arms up and out.

– Uh huh ho! he shouts. – Helloooooooooo!

He bounds back to the group. Judy swats at an oversized insect circling her head.

– Esme, says Granny, – take my hand and let's go look at some pretty flowers.

Esme tucks herself further into Baxter.

Granny tips her face down to Esme, her eyebrows crunched together in fury, terrible words about to topple from her lips.

Baxter crouches down, grasshopper-low, so he is eye to eye with Esme. He closes his eyes but bangs them open because of a smattering of nightmare about a lizard writhing in dust. – Granny wants you, Esme, he says.

He doesn't want to be here, in this place, among these trees, these jagged giant wedges of rock at a crossroads. They both should shelter inside the car.

– I need to clean up a little mess. Can you keep Granny company while I clean up a little spill?

The pink drops from Esme's face. She clamps her teeth into her own hand with the zeal of a dog biting into a human leg and digs her incisors in, grinding at her own meat and bones.

– Don't do that! says Granny, and she catches Esme by the elbows, shakes her. – I told you to stop it!

– Do you want to read my book some more? asks Baxter.

Ice crystals rise from the ground into the soles of his shoes.

She nods, her teeth still clamped into the back of her hand, the skin red and raw.

– Can you let go your hand? Even scarabs sometimes let go of their prey.

She glares at him, at Granny. Grandchild and grandmother mirror images of each other in their mutual, warped outrage.

He hands her the book. She unclamps her hand from her teeth only to reach for the book. Granny leads her to a tree knoll, and Esme walks in a circle, like a dog preparing to lie down, before she clumps down on the ground, traces the outline of the scarab lightly pressed into the cloth cover, the spiky legs. Opens the cover.

Granny studies Esme as though Esme is a wart on her hand. She pats the back of her own head, silver stripes throughout her hair, a twisted bun done up crooked at the back.

He steps up into the vestibule, into the car, to sweep up crushed crackers, as far away from the crossroad as he can get.

From a copse of spindly evergreens, a man with a face composed only of rings and rings of molars studies Baxter. Baxter pulls back, trying to obscure himself in the iron shadows of the train, dustpan in his hand. He rubs and rubs at his eyes, his eyes pink and wet as birds' mouths, cheeping for just one squiggly worm of sleep.

After sweeping the crushed crackers out of the carpet, he'll dust every corner and surface after all that prairie. If all the passengers leave his car, he'll try some covert push-ups, explode into a short stationary run to keep his blood pure. Count how many clean towels and sheets he has left, how many have been stolen and that he'll have to pay for and that will eat into the $974.47 he's saved up. Because if this train doesn't get moving soon, he'll have none left. If this train doesn't get moving, he will shrivel and die.

Passengers mill about outside the doors, gambolling in the mountain meadow; they duck in and out among the pines, stroll arm in arm, poke sticks at things in and among the pine needles, spongy moss, fallen branches, and tree trunks. Some of the men dip their feet in a small creek, the women their fingertips; they pick wildflowers, loudly admire the mountains (*There's still snow! It looks like decorations on a cake!*), brood and grumble about the lateness of the train.

Andrew Swain, in a dapper man's suit and taller than all of them, kohl and lipstick washed away, signs autographs in the middle of a clump of passengers, his lips wide and expressive around his unnaturally bright, large teeth, his voice booming loud enough that Baxter can hear it from inside his car. In between autographs he tells the Spider about a ghost who terrorized the cast on the set of his last motion picture. He tells her about a person he needs to contact, and she's the only person he can imagine helping him.

Andrew Swain, a world-famous *vaudeville performer and motion picture star* among them! His wavy blond hair glittering frosty in the sun.

His smile twists into pain when Judy grabs him by the arm and reminds him that her compartment is haunted.

Esme migrates to a tree stump directly across from the vestibule, Baxter's *The Scarab from Jupiter* open on her lap, running her finger along the lines of words as though reading. Granny walks behind her in an attitude of stony prayer. Judy skips up behind Granny, about to tap Granny on the shoulder. Baxter turns away.

Without the passengers, without Esme clinging to his back, without the rumble of the wheels on the track, the train is so quiet Baxter almost believes he can hear the rustle of the leaves in that bad patch of trees. His head nods asleep, then jerks back awake. The trembling man in his black socks creeps on his hands and knees among the sections, looking for something. The floor unsteady for a moment under Baxter's feet. Only a moment.

The Spider boards, alone. Stepping over the trembling man, she settles herself back into her seat.

axter marches back and forth down the aisle with the carpet sweeper. As long as he keeps walking from one end of the car to the other, he can stay awake. One foot in front of the other, the low swish of his pant legs as they brush back and forth against each other, the low squeak of the leather on his shoes, as the leather uppers pull at the worn soles, the whir of the sweeper brushing the same long strip, licking up the crumbs and fragments, his breath strongly in and out. Really, he shouldn't clean in front of a passenger, but the crackers crumbled and spread out everywhere into flour. The Spider ignores Baxter as she hunches over her half-embroidered scene. He steps back into a section as Judy sweeps into the car.

– What's that picture again? Judy asks the Spider, exhaling from exertion, her hands full of stringy purple flowers.

Baxter leans down and scrubs with his hand broom at the patch of crumbs, trying to sweep himself awake too. Was there jam on these crackers? Tears of vexation pool in his eyes. He stays crouched down, scrubbing at the carpet, close to weeping with his desire to lie on the ground and close his eyes.

– You've found some mountain asters, says the Spider.
Harebells.

– Well. I'm embroidering a radish dancing with a scallion.

– So creative, says Judy. – I was wondering. Might we have another sitting tonight?

His head drops, and he slams his head up again. Awake. He almost breathed in the water and drowned that time.

Judy dumps herself into the seat across from the Spider.

The Spider's needle squeaks in and out of the fabric.

– What did your spirit control mean last night about crossroads, asks Judy.

– We'd have to ask him.

Baxter starts picking out fine crumbs with his fingers.

– Can you see anything more about me? Can you see anything about this train?

The squeaking of the needle stops, and the long embroidery thread hisses as it passes through the fabric panel.

– Just one thing? asks Judy.

– All right, says the Spider. – I see the imprint of a woman's fingers over your heart.

– Oooh! says Judy, blushing. – Well. Hmm. And what about the train itself?

– No more, no less than any other place. Some ectoplasmic traces. The only definitive one is a formerly living porter who creeps around and among us in his pain.

Baxter stops picking.

– How frightening. How did he die?

His heart stutters.

– We'd have to ask my control to make contact.

– So thrilling! Could you have the porter speak to us?

The needle and thread continue their squeaking and hissing.

– Would you be able to conduct another séance? Could you find out what other phantasms inhabit this train?

– They exhaust me physically. I die inch by inch every time. I must charge a fee. Andrew Swain is also desperate for my help.

– Oh, says Judy. – Of course. Judy's voice drops. – Come outside. There's someone I want you to talk to.

The Spider stands, gently places the embroidery hoop on her seat, brushes stray embroidery thread strands from her lap, and follows Judy to the vestibule.

He sweeps busily as they file past him.

He peeks out the window.

The Spider steps down after Judy, Mad Mary guiding the Spider down the steps. She picks her way down, her limbs long and angled, her knees rising too high with each step. The women step off toward Esme and Granny.

He violently jams the carpet sweeper up and down the aisle. The sweeper head wheels and pokes into the sections, bumps into corners and along carpeted edging. The many-toothed man shifts to standing, still settled among the trees. What would happen if Baxter took dental pliers to the man's face? He's seen people with missing faces before. Tucked up in the highest branches of trees, peering out of legislature and shanty windows, shop door frames, outhouses, peppering riverbanks, sometimes even among the clouds, and clustering at crossroads, of course. As a child he would wake up so terrified he could not make a sound, alone in the searing dark, hearing nothing but the scream of crickets, but he couldn't tell his mother because she would say he was making up stories, and she wished *she* had time for stories, and then she would plump herself back to bed, didn't he know she had to wake up early in the morning for her job, shaking her head at this sissy child. He would shut his eyes as they passed through crossroads, pretend dust had flown into his eyes, or just say that he preferred his eyes closed right at that moment because he wanted to pray, Papa.

He bends down to pick at a melted jelly bean crusted to a baseboard. Only half the candy peels up with his fingernails, the rest stuck, the varnish on the wood peeling up with the sugar. A tiny horse escapes from a crack under the baseboard, rears on its tiny hind legs, and gallops off. He rubs his eyes.

When he was very small he told Aunt Arimenta about the people with no faces or queer faces that looked like teeth or like they'd been dead for a very long time, and when she nodded and blew pipe smoke out of the corner of her mouth like he was telling her about the weather yesterday, he told her more and more about the things he thought he saw. Her open face, her old-person wisdom.

– Ever since you were a baby you've been a bad sleeper, she said. – It's just your own sleepy clan, sugar. Find a way to get a good night's sleep and they'll go away. She held his chin and looked into his eyes, a thin trail of smoke twisting up from her pipe. – Why does the world have to be so small, she said. She tapped out her pipe against the breadfruit tree. – It's too small. Even these shoes are too small. It's far too small for people like you, my baby boy.

For many years, he was the only one with this affliction, with this taint of madness and ability to see the strange when he hadn't slept enough. And then he read a story in *Weird Tales*.

'The Revenants,' the writer titled the story.

Baxter scratched out a long letter to the writer, his pencil scraping out his insides as he unloaded his guts onto the pieces of paper. When he reached the bottom of the final page, he signed his name, then read and reread his words until tears sparked in his eyes. The writer never wrote back, no matter how many times he checked for a letter. Still, 'The Revenants' let him know he was not the only one.

A passenger screams.

A group of them pour and rush up into Baxter's car, trampling and jostling into the seats on the right side of the car.

Miss Tupper keens in her seat, rocking, her hand over her mouth. Judy sits beside her, gripping her around the shoulders.

– Well, that is a disturbing sight, says Mrs. Tupper, sliding her satiny bottom into her seat opposite Miss Tupper. As the Spider slides onto the flowery seat, the legs of her spidery hairpin tilt and glisten.

When the mist in the gorge burned away, Miss Tupper peered over the edge. The sun cut through the mist in the gorge, and the chasm revealed its hideous contents. A pile of train cars lay heaped at the bottom of the gorge.

– Fallen like that, says Miss Tupper, – over the *edge*. What about the passengers?

She yanks down the blind next to her. She jumps up and darts from section to section, pulling down the blinds in the car.

– Porter, help me!

Baxter holds back a sigh. He pulls down blind after blind.

Mad Mary strides in, frowning. – That was a very old train, miss, one from when they first laid down the track. There's no way a modern train like ours, with superior engineering and design, like this one, would have the same mishap. In fact, it's impossible, engineering-wise.

Mrs. Tupper purses her lips.

– Porter, she says, – we'll need smelling salts, I believe Carlotta's about to faint. Perhaps a little water.

– Tell me, says Miss Tupper, turning to the Spider. – Do you see or sense any of the poor souls down below?

– I must go into trance, says the Spider. – That is the only way we can know for certain.

The Spider lays her embroidery down on her lap, closes her eyes, crosses one ankle over the other, and leans back against the flowery upholstery.

– We must have another séance, says Judy, her arms around Miss Tupper. She reaches a hand to the Spider. – We must reach out to the deceased, give them comfort, ask them to see us through this part of the journey safely.

Mrs. Tupper frowns, and a vertical wrinkle etches between her eyebrows. – We could just light a candle and pray.

– Carlotta, direct communication with the spirits of the deceased will hearten you, says Judy to Miss Tupper, – I just know it. It does me. It's always such a comfort to speak with my mother who passed away from the flu. Our room will fit all if we don't mind getting close. She clasps her hands. – A grand idea.

She turns to the Spider.

– What shall we require for you to make contact? Will this be an ectoplasmic experience, you think?

– Who shall pay my fee? asks the Spider.

– We could all share in the fee, says Judy.

– We could? asks Mrs. Tupper.

– And perhaps we could contact baby Esme's deceased mother.

– And my cousin Morley! says Miss Tupper. – Morley was shot in the war.

She grabs her mother's arm. – Maybe I could speak to my father. He died when I was just a baby. I have so many questions!

She squeezes her mother's arm. A half smile sneaks onto her face.

– You were a widow and remarried, Mrs. Tupper? asks the Spider. She traces a finger around the edge of her hoop.

Mrs. Tupper flips open a handkerchief and fans herself violently, the wrinkle in her forehead even deeper. – I'm going back outside.

She bumps her hip into a seat in her haste to leave.

– Onward to my Drawing Room! Judy declares. – We'll need you, Porter, says Judy.

A flowerlet inlaid into a walnut panel above Baxter's head blooms then wilts.

The Spider trails the women as they troop, single file, down the tubular passageway to the Drawing Room, their lacy elbows, their soft, pink hands trailing and tapping along the polished wood panelling, the flowery wood inlays.

Sunlight squeaks in around the edges of the blinds; it is, after all, only just after midday, and Baxter cringes at the dust motes slipping in and out of the light beams in the Drawing Room, the curls of chilly air that slither down the walls. In this room, he feels the stoniness, the silence of his parents' house, the smell of perpetual disappointment. He can barely stand it, idling here in this room that oozes so much melancholy.

The Spider stows herself in Punch and Judy's private WC. Miss Tupper and Judy sit holding hands across from each other in the gloom. Baxter stands with his rump against the wall.

Nothing but the sound of their breathing. Judy sniffs.

The WC door stays closed.

Miss Tupper clears her throat. Judy rubs her thumb on Miss Tupper's thumb and raises her eyebrows.

A fragment of a passenger's voice glimmers outside. A bird trills. Another bird answers. The mountains hulk around them. Magma twists far below the train tracks.

Judy sniffs twice.

A bang in the lavatory.

Baxter jumps. Miss Tupper gasps, Judy chortles.

Inside the lavatory, the Spider drones out a low moan.

The Spider starts to whistle a song. Saucily, unbecomingly.

A tune Edwin Drew used to whistle. Baxter's heart beats faster. Too fast.

– Hello, sweet ladies, a husky voice says from behind the door.

– Is this Victor? asks Judy.

Silence.

– I will ask again, says Judy, – is this Victor, Mrs. Crane's deceased brother? Mrs. Crane's spirit control?

– What a goddamn stupid question, says the Spider.

Judy hops in her seat with excitement.

– Christ, I'm thirsty, says the Spider. – Who does a man need to pull off to get a beer around here?

Miss Tupper gasps.

– Victor can be coarse sometimes, Judy whispers to Miss Tupper. – I learned that last night during my private consultation.

– I see … , says Victor from inside the lavatory, – I see the words *Merry Widow*.

– Must be the operetta? says Miss Tupper.

– And a friend who loves you dearly.

– How sweet, says Miss Tupper.

Baxter backs himself deep into the corner.

The Spider wolf-whistles. – Carlotta, Carlotta, why don't we marry? Give me a kiss, Carlotta. Could I ever use a kiss.

– Repulsive, whispers Miss Tupper.

– But maybe you could try it? whispers Judy back.

Judy flaps her hands at Miss Tupper, flaps them at Baxter, then back at Miss Tupper.

– Ooooooh, moans Victor lustily.

– Victor can be somewhat common, whispers Judy. – As I learned last night. Mrs. Crane says they were very close growing up, but when he died, well, death made him resentful of the living. He's a little jealous of his sister, Mrs. Crane, I think.

– A coloured man wants to speak with you, Carlotta, sweet Carlotta, says Victor behind the door.

– What's the man want to say? asks Judy, her fingers choking Miss Tupper's, her eyes wide. – What does he want? Why would he want to speak with Carlotta?

A bang comes from inside the door again.

– What about the poor souls in the gorge, Victor? asks Judy. – Are they in terrible torment? Do they require our help? Can you ask them to ensure we have safe passage through these mountains?

– The man is speaking, says the Spider.

– But what about the dead passengers in the gorge?

The door to the WC opens, and the Spider steps out slowly, her eyes drifting toward nothing, her hands in front of her. She halts. Falls to her hands and knees. Opens her mouth. A creamy spew sails onto the carpet, splashing her hands. Baxter grits his teeth. Another goddamn mess!

Judy rushes forward with a hanky and scrubs at the Spider's mouth. A sick, syrupy smell saturates the small room.

– Teleplasm! says Judy, leaning down and poking a fingertip into the spew. – How terribly exciting!

Or just plain old porridge with far too much cream, thinks Baxter. He can even spot a whole blueberry in the mess.

– Oh, gags Miss Tupper, her hands over mouth. – I'm going to be *sick*.

Her face turns bright red, then drains right away, her freckles bright against her suddenly chalky skin.

– I'll clean that up right away, madam, says Baxter.

– Are you hearing anything from the people at the bottom of the gorge? asks Judy, her hands grabbing the sides of the Spider's pale, sweaty face. – Victor, speak to me. Can you hear my mother?

Victor belches, raucous, long, in Judy's face. – I don't give a fig about your mother. Your mother's in the ground.

– Victor, can you hear the people in the gorge?

Judy is almost shouting now. She leans forward. – What killed the coloured man who's here for Carlotta? she asks. – What's his name?

– I don't want to speak with Victor or the man, wails Miss Tupper.

Baxter wobbles; the only thing keeping him from fainting is the wall behind him.

Miss Tupper bursts into tears.

Baxter rushes out the door and down the passageway to the cupboard for rags to mop up the regurgitated porridge. Where's Mad Mary? Out the window, against the backdrop of the mountains with their veins of snow, Templeton confabs with Mad Mary and Stanley the engineer. Of course Mad Mary's off socializing instead of doing his job.

Baxter turns on his heel, back to the Drawing Room. The bell on his call board rings. He pirouettes, not sure which direction to go. And he needs to use the toilet!

Hour 96. At breakfast, crowded behind their curtain, neither Baxter nor the other porters talk while they eat, not Ferdinand, not Freckles, not A.P., not even Templeton. Their somnolence sits crammed with them at the small table, forcing them to the very edges. The aching silence of the train, the stillness as they drag themselves down the halls of this opulent string of bedrooms on wheels. Cold cereal migrates too slowly from Baxter's spoon and down his throat, into his gullet. He has only shreds of brown shoe-shine left, and now he's running low on black too. Will he still have to pay for this food, even though the train being late is not his fault? The money he costed out for meals has been dribbling and evaporating. Five towels have vaporized, gone, and that's going to cost him. He didn't budget for an extra day-and-a-half-two-days-he's-lost-count-of-the-days-long hell in the mountains. He didn't budget for accumulating demerits and diminishing tips as the passengers grow more angry.

In the creeping morning light, in the bushes – because Mad Mary finally took mercy on the porters and allowed them all off the oppressively stuffy train for a reprieve – he tries to jolt himself awake by leaping into calisthenic exercises. He huffs and puffs into star-shaped leaps, push-ups, squats, lunging with first one leg then the other, but he wobbles as he moves, his legs shifting with the automatic, phantom movements of a travelling train. He closes his eyes for only a second and a tiny dream pops up of him lying on an impossibly soft mattress perfect for the princess and her pea and her pea's pea. Templeton wanders by, fanning himself with a time-table in the heat. Through a green fork of bush, Mad Mary and Ferdinand confer about something farther up the train, and Baxter ducks further into the bushes, a branch digging into his elbow. He hopes he hasn't soiled his white jacket. He brought three shirts on this run. He'll get demerits for grime collecting on the shirts after days and days, even if he manages to keep stains off them. Damn. His shoulders sag. He splashes his face with cold, fresh water from the mountain creek. He drinks melting glacier, plunges his hands into the water past the point of ice just to wake himself up and calm himself down. He ascends into the vestibule, his legs shaky, his hands icy numb.

The train is two nights late, less two hours. He wonders if the porter whose shift he's covering has recovered from the pneumonia, and how that porter will manage the loss of money, the growing stain of unreliability that attaches itself to every instance he falls sick. Or perhaps the porter has lain in bed this whole time, still sleeping after ninety-six hours.

He says hello to Dr. Hubble from Compartment B as he steps up into the train.

– Nice day, says Dr. Hubble. He knocks his forehead on a door frame.

This run will never end. Baxter parks himself in the WC, his insides feverish and bursting.

He pulls the postcard out of his pocket. Unfolds it. He finally allows his hand to grip his crotch, his fingers to unbutton his fly.

The door jerks open. Baxter jerks back into the wall. The postcard thunks to the floor.

Dr. Hubble locks eyes with him for less than a second, and Baxter stares right back. Dr. Hubble shuts the door behind him.

Quickly, Dr. Hubble's hand cups Baxter's hand, presses into Baxter, rubs Baxter's cock. Baxter removes his hand from himself, rubs the Doctor back.

– I've seen you kick the walls, you know, gasps the Doctor.

Baxter's tongue is too thick to speak.

They move silently, they breathe into each other's mouths, their teeth clash as Baxter kisses him, eager to tongue his teeth, the doctor's skin wet under Baxter's fingers, Baxter's fingers dark against this white man's lethal pink skin.

Baxter lets himself fall backward, disappear.

In less than a few moments they are spent, their hands wet with each other's semen. Baxter wipes his hands, straightens his jacket. He grabs the postcard. Exits into the empty passageway, his blood sizzling, his hips liquid from the sudden release.

At the end of the passageway, next to the smoker, his bell rings.

– Beyond. Belief, says Punch, champing a mouthful of jelly beans.

– Your sister will have a fit, says Judy. – She'll think we somehow did this on purpose. She'll find a way to blame it on me, I just know it, the old buzzard.

– Now we'll never get the money.

– What money? asks Judy.

For the first time, heat rises in her cheeks.

– You rang the bell, madam? Sir? asks Baxter.

– You don't need to know, says Punch.

– What money?

Tears glint in her eyes, and she reaches her hands out to Punch.

The Drawing Room door slams shut. Baxter bustles away.

Back in her section, Miss Tupper's eyes punch red holes in her face. She dabs her nose with an embroidered handkerchief.

The passengers foment in their restlessness.

This interminable run. This train that for some reason refuses to *train*, parked at the edge of a death gorge, in the middle of a crossroad.

axter stands, running his dust rag over an inlaid walnut wood flower on a wall panel again and again. His arm is the only limb he can move. He has fallen asleep standing up, he has fallen asleep and in his sleep he continues to tend to the train. He wants to tear out his own throat.

Late afternoon now. Ladies sitting delicately on blankets in the meadow, their boredom and cabin fever grown so powerful it has overwhelmed their fear of the deaths in the gorge. They picnic on crustless pumpernickel, egg, and watercress sandwiches packed specially by the chef, while men smoke and wave their arms wide, strutting their strength. Haggard waiters step among them with trays of tea and coffee and the occasional wine or whisky glass, their white jackets gleaming in the late sunshine. Pulp and Paper confab to the side, their heads down, their lips and jaws chewing furiously as they talk.

The person whose face is only teeth has perched himself high up in a pine tree.

A man seated among a clump of passengers smokes a cigarette and sips from a cocktail glass, laughs so hysterically at a joke one of them tells, his drink slops.

Esme still studies *The Scarab from Jupiter* as though she can understand the words. She has apparently read three-quarters of the way through. Soon night will fall and she will climb up onto his back again.

The dust cloth warm under his hand, the wooden flower slowly blooming as he rubs off microscopic layers of varnish. In another part of the train, Dr. Hubble's pen nib squeaks a letter to his friend David in a jail cell.

The clink and whistle of voices in the vestibule. Two women, arguing.

– *It's nobody's business but ours*, one of the voices says, as he opens the door to the vestibule.

Mrs. Tupper holds Miss Tupper by the shoulders, their foreheads touching. He nods hello at the Tuppers as he passes them in the vestibule. – Good afternoon, Mrs. and Miss Tupper, he says.

Airing their grievances in a hot vestibule seems strange because they seem to have no problem expressing themselves everywhere else in public. He has no problem imagining them coming to blows in the middle of the mountain meadow, rolling among the clover and bear dung. But now they stand in an eerie, dangerous silence. As he passes, the women turn from each other and register his intrusion, and the moment pauses, passes too slowly, passes like he is pacing through swamp, the two women side by side. The mother's eyes hazel, the daughter's eyes brown like her freckles. Not ginger-hair freckles.

They do not answer him as he passes.

He pulls open the door to the next car. Steps through.

– Porter!

He turns around. Mrs. Tupper.

Miss Tupper peeks around from behind her.

– What's your name? Mrs. Tupper asks.

– Stop it! says Miss Tupper.

– R.T., his voice creaks. – R.T. Baxter, madam.

– Well, my name is Sylvia, Mr. Baxter, and this is my daughter, Carlotta. I wanted to ask you something, Mr. Baxter –

– I said stop it! says Carlotta, grabbing her elbow, jerking her back. – Mother!

– The man Carlotta knows as her father is not her father at all. And maybe that's unusual, but I personally don't see anything wrong with that.

– Certainly, madam? he asks.

Carlotta yanks her mother toward her and slaps her. Carlotta's face gorges with blood. Her face contorts into sobs.

Sylvia hugs Carlotta tight.

He crushes the timetable in his pocket.

Sylvia hustles Carlotta toward the door leading outside. They pass by him from inside to outside.

Carlotta and her abundantly freckled nose. Her brown eyes so brown they are almost black, look straight into his as they pass by him.

D rops explode from the sky. The rain crashes down outside the windows, spatters and dribbles down the increasingly steamy glass. Cupping, sometimes grabbing, unsteady arms, elbows, hands, he helps passengers climb up into the train as the downpour pries the sky open. Pulp yabbers on about the unexpected weather patterns on this part of the continent as he pops up into the vestibule; Judy talks about how it must surely be the restless spirits in the gorge expressing their discontent as she clutches at Baxter's hand and he pushes her upward. The Spider boards next. Small purple flower petals confetti the women's hair, scatterings of pine needles stick to the men's clothes, their fingers sticky with sharp-smelling sap. The hem of the Spider's long, old-fashioned skirt is grimy with forest floor.

Dr. Hubble clambers up and Baxter reaches for his hand to help him up. Their hands clasp.

– Thank you, Porter, says Dr. Hubble.

Esme climbs up onto Baxter's back, her hands grasping his Adam's apple, and the two of them glide up into the vestibule's dark metal hull.

Punch gave up long ago on asking anyone he could when the train will start moving again. Baxter brings him a coffee in the Drawing Room. Old Punch twiddles his thumbs on his generous belly. He has placed his sticky palm on the misty window, the handprint still there, the raindrops drizzling down. Baxter almost feels sorry for him missing his sister in Sicamous. But probably this plum pudding–shaped man is so rich, he could buy away the rain if he chose to.

Back by the smoker, his bell rings. The Tuppers.

– You rang, miss?

– Porter, asks Carlotta.

– It's Mr. Baxter, interrupts her mother. – Mr. Baxter has a name just like the rest of us.

– George, says Carlotta, – my head feels like there is a thunderstorm inside it. Do you have any headache powder?

Click. Click click. Click.

– His name isn't George! You know better, Carlotta Tupper, you know better, Mrs. Tupper says.

Carlotta pauses. She clutches her stomach, her breaths short and sharp.

– What do you mean, she knows better? asks the Spider, shedding pine needles in a circle.

The interior of his car is humid, a wet wool coat draped over everyone's shoulders. Even the prattling of passengers dies down as their car languishes on the siding an eternity longer than eternity. Baxter sits on his stool. *In the bicuspids the buccal half of the crown is quite similar to the crown of the cuspid* he licked the Doctor's bicuspids, that's how far in Baxter shoved his tongue *but in the lingual half a complete revolution has taken place.* His body no longer fits him, his arms too jangly, his neck floppy. Probably the Doctor will try to find an excuse to get him fired. Desperate feelings can swivel into loathing.

Outside the window, a moose licks the wet glass, its thick tongue trailing behind a giant slug trail. It licks and sucks the sill. But the moose must be standing on stilts or levitating, yet another hallucination. Baxter stands up, turning away from the giant head gnawing on the other side of the glass as he rubs a cloth back and forth on the fingerprinted woodwork around the window. Wild roses formed of sliced wood. He too, formed of sliced wood. Glued together and polished with moose saliva. It all makes sense.

Esme rubs a baseboard with a green cloth.

That night, most of the passengers settle into their berths without fuss. No one asks for an extra or a different pillow, no one spills. The symphony of snoring and sighs starts up almost immediately, louder now as the train's engine continues its excruciating stillness.

He shines shoes, scraping off mud and pine needles, shreds of moss, and globules of drying sap. Esme buffs her own little boots. Slaps on bootblack.

His bell rings.

– Porter, pronounces Judy importantly, standing in the doorway, – Victor has determined there is indeed a spirit. Whether it is a spirit that resides on this train or *someone else*, Victor has not specified. It would be useful to have little Esme present.

Judy withdraws into the crowded Drawing Room, the compartment big but not *that* big, the chill wisping in the corners, dripping down from the ceiling.

Esme perches in his arms, her body tense, twitchy.

The Drawing Room smells of candle wax, scorched candle wick, and human breath. Punch, Judy, Granny sit wedged in, long past midnight, Judy and Granny wearing shawls.

In the WC, Victor whistles a line from the song 'Souvenir.'

Baxter breathes in deeply, hunting for the reassuring and steady smell of a pine tree outside to help him escape this room, or the cold powder of a blasted-out stone wall, a minor waterfall trickling in the bushes, even a grain elevator far, far away. Anything but his own sorry smell.

All these people should be asleep in their fancy beds.

One of Esme's hair ribbons lies rippled across Judy's lap.

These monsters.

– The little girl's mother, whispers Victor from inside the WC.

– Dead by her own hand! yells Victor.

Baxter claps his hands over Esme's eyes, her ears. Granny gasps and leaps up to standing, bumping over the others to pull Esme out of Baxter's arms. Esme screams, kicking away her grandmother, clinging with her arms around Baxter's neck.

The Spider mumbles in the closet in her own voice. – I can't seem to open this door, she says. – Help me, someone.

Judy applauds, delighted.

They should have pulled into Vancouver days ago. In the empty diner, Mad Mary stands over the porters' table while they gnaw through stale currant buns, and he ticks off a list in his hand with a pencil, tells them that passengers in the sections can't have showers because there isn't enough water, and if the train still isn't running in the morning, it would be useful if they could put on a concert for the passengers, sing or dance or play musical instruments, anyone know any songs? – Could we do a chorus? Put on a concert?

– I'm going to ask Mr. Swain if he'll kindly put on a vaudeville show for us, says Mad Mary. – Entertainers love doing that.

They chew as Mad Mary describes his wonderful plan. Baxter is glad he has no talents. Esme chews a piece of bacon at his feet under the table, which will make Granny happy.

– I've got my trumpet, says Templeton.

– You've got your harmonica, says Mad Mary to Ferdinand.

– I suppose, says Ferdinand.

– Or perhaps you could do a kite-flying demonstration.

– No wind.

– I've seen you fly that kite without a stick of wind.

– But … but … , says Ferdinand.

– Too complicated, says Mad Mary. – Baxter, could you dance the Black Bottom while we play? You must know how to do the Black Bottom.

Esme crawls out from under the table and leans against Baxter. She takes a giant bite of her bacon, chews. Buttery cookie crumbs stick to her cheek.

– Don't know the Black Bottom. Don't dance, says Baxter, looking down at the top of Esme's dishevelled head.

Her hair needs a comb.

– Don't dance or can't dance? says Mad Mary. – What the devil do you mean?

– Mmm hmmm, says Baxter.

– Don't dance or can't dance, repeats Mad Mary, lifting his lips and showing his teeth.

– Can't, says Baxter. – Two left feet!

He yawns. One after the other, they all yawn, even Mad Mary.

Esme's lips stick out as she chews a final bit of fat, twists her tongue to swish back and forth at a raisin wedged between her two front teeth.

Mad Mary turns to A.P. – Can you dance?

A.P.'s chin falls out of his hand, and he jerks his head up, blinking away sleep.

– Where are we? rasps A.P.

– Oh forget it, says Mad Mary.

Out in the mountain meadow, the rain from last night still glittering around them, the audience claps along appreciatively, their ringed, well-fed hands dazzling in the afternoon. They laze on blankets in the clearing, the sun sharp and angry.

Ferdinand tries and fails to raise his kite up in flight, his face sweaty and like he might just start crying. He trips more than once, the red kite thunking over and over into the ground.

Andrew Swain sings 'Me and the Boyfriend' in a high falsetto in his grass-green dress, his lips glossy red, a sculpted golden wig rippling close to his head. The audience laughs when he sings out the line, *I'm only twenty, and he's fifty-threeee*, and Baxter claps too.

– And now, Judy announces, – the 'Flower Duet' from *Lakme*.

She knots her hands together. Andrew Swain reaches his hands out to her, draws his face close to hers, and gently pulls her hands apart.

He nods. She nods back.

Their voices ripple, opera bright.

Andrew Swain's voice twines and dances with Judy's, Judy transformed into a laughing flower until the final, hovering note.

The audience's claps thonk amidst the trees, bounce over the small creek.

– Next up, announces Mad Mary, – Porter Templeton!

He sweeps his arms wide. Templeton steps his shiny shoes up onto a disintegrating tree trunk and buzzes his lips. He smiles to the left, then to the right. He lifts the gold horn up to his lips. The first note peals in the amphitheatre of mountains.

Tears start in Baxter's eyes at the golden sound of Templeton's breath.

As a finale, Mad Mary encourages all of them – passengers, porters, waiters, engineer, brakeman, fireman – to sing 'God Save the King.' Mad Mary sings raucously, his voice louder than everyone's.

Baxter taps his palms against his thighs, but he only whispers the words and tries not to see the sideways glances of Punch and Judy at his whispering. He sways, stumbles, rights himself.

– Falling asleep on the job I see, says Judy, and she laughs.

Carlotta Tupper stands off to the side. Her arms crossed, she doesn't applaud when the singing stops, even when her mother pinches her hip.

Dr. Hubble laughs and talks with Mad Mary, with Punch, with passengers from other cars. He has a damp spot on his bottom from where he must have accidentally sat on a wet log. He looks at everyone but Baxter.

A shout erupts from the forest behind them.

Pulp and Paper erupt from the trees, Pulp pulling Paper's shirt over his head, Paper's arms flailing, Paper punching Pulp in the crotch. They flump to the ground and roll, hands slapping, arms and legs flinging and kicking.

Andrew Swain leaps after the men, holding his skirts high, and clumps their heads together. – Not! During! A! Show! he says.

Mad Mary yanks Pulp away by an elbow, Andrew Swain sits on Paper, Pulp and Paper's noses bleeding, hair askew, and Pulp's face filthy from where Paper likely ground his face into the mud, their collars popped.

Pulp's face has a long scratch down the side. Their knees and elbows are mottled with grass stains, the crowns of their heads studded with flower petals.

N ight sets again.

Granny drags Esme away, Esme bawling.

He sweeps one of the vestibules because pine needles have scattered all over the floor. One of the vestibule doors punches open. Judy, in tears, followed by Punch, who is reaching his hand out to her.

– I want to go home, Judy says, pushing away Punch's hand. She tugs on the other vestibule door. – I don't care about Sicamous.

Punch whispers, – My dear, we have no choice but to care about Sicamous.

He pulls the door open for her.

– Why? asks Judy. – Why didn't you tell me before?

The door shuts behind them.

Baxter's bell rings. Baxter shakes out the broom before he tends to the bell. When he reaches the call board, the arrow next to Compartment B is askew. Dr. Hubble's room.

His fingers tremble as he presses the small circle by the door.

Neither of them speaks. No *You rang, sir?* No *Fetch me a drink, Porter.*

The Doctor reaches for one of Baxter's hands and holds on the way they did earlier, but longer. The electric shock, the thrill of skin against skin. Baxter pulls the Doctor toward him, and they collide, Baxter breathing in his odour, the Doctor burying his face in Baxter's neck.

He shouldn't be in here. Sixty demerits. He will end his life in a jail cell. Zero dollars saved. At best Baxter will end up working on freight trains for not even half the pay. He shouldn't let the man tug at the buttons on his fly. Baxter puts his hands on the Doctor's shoulders as though to push him away, his skin craves skin, he will spend the rest of his life in jail.

Edwin Drew.

Baxter hopes the Doctor doesn't pay him, or give him an extra-generous tip, or a bill torn in half. The Doctor's mouth tugging with outrageous skill, like he has done this many times before. Maybe Baxter is only a man-shaped piece of furniture for him. Useful. Baxter tries not to let go. He feels the graze of the Doctor's teeth on his cock, which pushes him off the cliff, he careens with aching pleasure, headfirst to the bottom.

He forgets Edwin Drew. But only for a moment.

G ranny's bell rings. Esme has won. Again.
– She won't stop kicking me, says Granny.

With Esme back at his side, he's not sure what she sees and what she does not, and he's not sure he cares anymore, he opens the linen locker to fetch more towels. The trembling man has wedged himself into the bottom shelf, his teeth chattering. The man is Baxter. Baxter the man. The man in the linen locker stops chattering, the sound lessening until it nearly disappears.

He sags on his stool, Esme at his feet with cards.

He startles. Esme, who was at his feet, has disappeared, his eyeglasses hang from one ear, and his jacket sags open at the chest. He taps his chest, feeling his pockets. The postcard. The pocket lies loose, just an empty silken envelope. The postcard.

He bounds to his feet, dashes from the washroom, his heart glaciered in his chest, perhaps he should just throw himself out the vestibule door right now, straight into the gorge.

In the passageway, Esme stands on her tiptoes, a soft whine in her throat as she reaches up to Granny's hands as Granny reads the picture on Baxter's postcard. Judy stands there too, the door to the Drawing Room ajar, the Spider's head peeping out. They all study the postcard. Their heads swivel as one to Baxter. He has lost his job, he has lost his life.

Footsteps tap behind him, and Mrs. Tupper appears in her shimmering kimona, a paper cup of water in her hand.

She laughs.

– What's all this? she asks. – Why's everyone still awake?

She pushes past Baxter and picks the postcard out of Granny's hands.

– My, she says. – My my my.

– What's going on? she asks Baxter.

– Someone left it at the first stop, he says. – I found it in the car. When I was cleaning.

– I'll have you fired, says Granny, grabbing Esme's shoulders, gathering Esme to her, Granny's mouth jammed to the brim with teeth so sharp, so yellow, they look like little animals.

Esme squirms, and Granny slaps her in the head, Esme's hair fluttering. Esme hunches into a gargoyle, her pupils contracting into slits.

– Well! says Mrs. Tupper.

– Esme thieved, says Granny, her mouth souring. – But this boy! This wickedness, the evil nonsense I hear him pouring into her ears about man-sized beetles and Mars.

Click click click. Boy boy boy. Clickety click. He is an automaton click click clicking hands clicking teeth clicking feet click click click clicking knees clickety clickety click. He is a clicking George clicking clickety how can I help you click sir click boy click lady click click.

His teeth chatter.

– This? asks Mrs. Tupper, holding up the postcard. – But this is nothing. It's only Greek Love. The ancient Greeks venerated the male body in this very same way, she says, slapping the postcard against a palm. – What nonsense. This is *my* postcard. I was using it as a bookmark. Here, she says to Baxter, handing it to him. – Since these people are so offended by the natural beauty of the human body, I'm sure you know what to do with this.

– I haven't slept one minute since my daughter died, says Granny. – I am sick to the back teeth of being on this train. My daughter was too young to die. I want to go home. I want my poodle Nelson. I want a sherry, I want my own bed. My daughter was too young to die.

Granny's entire self distorts into grief, into rage, into embarrassment, into grandmother-gargoyle sleep hallucination, into a rat-king emotion only Aunt Arimenta would know how to decipher.

The last time Baxter saw Edwin Drew. Leaving a Toronto barbershop, the shop glowing with light the colour of fire.

In a laneway. In the dark. Baxter walking by himself down Yonge Street, then Edwin with his new haircut smoothly following behind him in step. Baxter turning onto Albert Street, then into Albert Street lane. Edwin turned into the Albert lane too.

Standing together, huddled in the shadow of an Eaton's warehouse, Edwin's arm over his shoulder, their hands gripping and stroking each other, their knees weak, when the policeman's voice erupted. Baxter's hands wet with Edwin Drew, his fingers dripping with love.

The voice's blast in his skull.

Baxter ran.

His lungs fevered and blistering, his feet skimming packed dirt, spur tracks, wooden boardwalks, bricks locked into dusty, elaborate puzzles as he rounded corners, streaked past the department store, past warehouses, past more factories, running and running even after the pummelling footsteps behind him evaporated. He ripped off his eyeglasses as he ran so he wouldn't lose them, clutched them until the wires twisted, the streets and lights and people blurring as he swerved around them, nicked and bumped them with his shoulders, his elbows, shouting, he ran until the gassy street lights disappeared, he ran into the dark, he ran into the trees, he ran onto the tracks, he crouched on the tracks heaving for breath, his forehead down on his knees, until he heard the low whistle of a train, and he leapt away.

In the darkness, he disappeared.

In the darkness, Edwin Drew disappeared.

Edwin Drew was popular and sociable and upstanding and a good Christian and laughed too loudly with his big, perfect teeth and his flawless occlusion. Baxter was a nobody with bad eyes and central incisors that didn't line up with his lateral incisors, who seemed interested only in books about Martians and *Weird Tales*. Edwin Drew, forty. Married, his wife and children moving in with her brother, Eugene Grady. Edwin Drew a Baptist man. Incarcerated with two hundred dollars bail that his family couldn't afford, his name blaring in the newspaper so that everyone in the world could see it and know it.

Baxter read and reread his books and magazines about the deep sea and Martians and outer space and time travel and immortal beings and phantoms. He ate alone. He ironed his shirts. He shined his shoes so they glittered like stars when he walked. He circled the planet Earth in his spaceship, he flew up high on the back of giant scarabs from Jupiter, he travelled the oceans in submarines. He rested in the cellar of his castle in his box of dirt, friends with vermin. He sat on his chair in the speeding train, his back perfectly straight, and he slept with his eyes open, hallucinations draping his face, a tittering insect instead of a heart.

Edwin Drew: the best Porter Instructor in the country, he played poker like he invented it, slapping down his cards and shouting himself into a win.

– Behave on a train like an automaton at a carnival, Edwin Drew once said, straightening Baxter's collar. – Find that smile, the bigger the better, and push the button, turn it on, but don't Uncle Tom it. Don't *grin*. Sing, dance, do magic tricks if they ask you. Maybe other things if the money's worth it, but don't Uncle Tom. *So much easier, so little fuss. Bigger tips.* Sometimes I've sung, sometimes I've danced. Sometimes I've been ridden like a horse. So what? The tips I get? So what?

Baxter has no idea where Edwin Drew is now.

Baxter sweeps up a mummified fly flipped dead on its back on the floor of the linen closet, legs kinked, its blue belly glistening. He picks it up with his index finger and thumb.

Fly on the wall. He is no fly, although he has dealt in shit. He can feel he's smiling so stupidly, sleep slathering him, dragging him down.

And just like that, Mad Mary tells him, the two of them standing in the smoker, that he's fired.

– You're out as soon as we get to Banff, says Mad Mary.

And that's all Mad Mary says before he moves on with his life, with his wage, with his job.

Baxter sits down, starts shaking. He sits and shakes, his teeth chatter for a long, long time. The bell rings, but he keeps sitting because he cannot move his legs.

– Aren't you coming for breakfast? asks Ferdinand, emerging from the shadows.

– I'm not hungry, says Baxter.

– That's bunkum, says Ferdinand. – Come on.

– I'm running out of money. I can't afford to eat off that menu anymore.

– Come *on*, says Ferdinand.

Baxter enters the diner with the other porters. He takes a piece of bread.

– What else'll you have? asks Ferdinand. – You can't order less than twenty-five cents.

Templeton clears his throat. – Take the ham and eggs, man, he barks.

– I don't have the money, whispers Baxter. – I'm not hungry.

– We'll pay for your breakfast, says Ferdinand.

– Sure, says Freckles.

– Yes, says Templeton, sipping his coffee. – Mr. Magruder told me.

– We heard you found a French postcard, says Ferdinand.

– Hmph, says A.P.

Mad Mary marches by.

– Mr. Magruder, says Ferdinand.

– What is it?

– Some prankster's been leaving naughty postcards about the train.

– Yes, I *know*. The criminal's right there.

– But he told us he found his the same way we did. I found a postcard too, Templeton says. – Awful thing.

– No you didn't, says Mad Mary.

– So did I, says Freckles. – Some prankster's left them about the train.

– Where are they? says Mad Mary, frowning. – Give them to me.

– I threw mine out immediately.

– So did I. Out the window, in fact.

– This one here decided to keep his, says Mad Mary. – A passenger found it. Reported him. Out of my hands.

– Smart fella. Wish I'd done that, says Templeton.

– What? says Magruder.

– That's a really smart thing to do, says Ferdinand.

– What? asks Magruder. – He's fired. You're fired, Baxter. You're out of this company.

– Evidence! says Ferdinand. – So we can catch the perpetrator.

Mad Mary stands, his tongue boiling in his mouth, his teeth clenching and unclenching.

– I oughta fire all of you.

– Guess you might have to, says Templeton. – We can finally catch up on some sleep while we're stuck here in the mountains.

He guffaws so hard, coffee jiggles out of his cup.

– Jesus Christ, says Mad Mary, crossing his arms. – Archie, he says to Templeton, uncrossing his arms, holding out his hands, – what are you doing?

Templeton sips his coffee, his eyes shrunken and bloodshot, past waking, past sleeping.

– All right, Mad Mary says, holding a fist in one hand.

Templeton slurps. But his cup tremors.

– All right, Mad Mary says, punching the fist into the hand.
– You're not fired.

– Who's not fired? asks Templeton.

Baxter falls to the floor. He bangs his cheek into the floor. His hat flies from his head in a surprised arc.

Ammonia razors up into his nose.

– Get up, man! For God's sake, you can't lie *here*.

Mad Mary jerks Baxter back and forth, smelling salts in his other hand.

Baxter's stomach, his heart, has exploded.

Templeton sits back on his heels. – You fainted, he says, his voice matter-of-fact.

Baxter jerks himself up to sitting, climbs the side of a chair with his hands, clambers up to his feet where he stands, wobbling. The light from the windows too bright.

– I'm tip-top, Baxter says. – Tip-top. Never better.

He smiles, cracking his face in half at the other porters.

– If you say so, says Mad Mary. – Eat and then get back to work.

The day drags, the mountains hulk around them. Passengers cluster to the observation car to watch a brown bear and her two babies foraging. – DO NOT DETRAIN, says Mad Mary. – I REPEAT. DO NOT DETRAIN.

Later on, four deer stroll by, stiff-legged.

The car abruptly shudders, and the trees, the meadow, the gorge, gradually slide away. Passengers give jagged hurrahs and huzzahs, they applaud, some men whistle. Mrs. Tupper does too.

The Spider with her sparkly spider barrette huddles close to the window, as though she would like at any moment to jump out of it. Mrs. Tupper lounges with a wilting crown of purple mountain flowers in her hair. Carlotta Tupper chirps in a little girl's voice as she plays a fierce game of rummy on a little table with Paper, and Paper smiles shyly. Pulp hulks in the corner, a hat pulled down low over his face because he drank too much last night. Granny reads Baxter's copy of *The Scarab from Jupiter* with the tip of her smallest finger between her teeth; she asked to borrow it when Mrs. Tupper dared her to read it. She has read nothing like it, and she can think of nothing else. Baxter hopes she remembers to give it back to him, she will probably forget and pack it in her bag and what can he do about that? Nothing.

In Compartment A, Andrew Swain unpins his wig and wipes lipstick off his lips, rouge and powder off his cheeks, kohl from around his eyes with cold cream, but he does not remove his pink corset. He will go to the writing room and write a letter to his wife, Cicely, the way Mrs. Crane the medium advised. He misses the way Cicely could turn even the worst incident into a funny story, how she understood his ways and his friends. Now he's missed his show in Vancouver. He wishes he could tell her the story of this terrible train trip and have her tell it back to him. As soon as he gets to Vancouver, he is turning right around first thing so he can go back home to Cicely and lay the letter on her grave.

Suddenly, he feels the cold soles of her little feet on the small of his back. Her habit on winter nights. – Cicely? he asks, his heart bursting.

Esme and Rocky lie wedged between the sofa and Baxter's back. He lies on the sofa in the smoker. Her eyes melt closed but not quite closed, her arms around her horse. Baxter's bell does not ring. He dozes, but he is the waking dead, he feels a burst of waking energy, he is a revenant, but for once the thing deep in him feels sated, even if only for a short time.

His eyes dry as a mountain peak.

In Banff, Baxter helps off the Tupper mother and daughter, a plain white hat on Carlotta's head. The daughter presses a fifty-cent piece into his palm as though it is Aladdin's treasure. Then she turns away, off to her cancelled wedding.

Mrs. Tupper stuffs a wedge of tightly folded bills into his palm. She winks at him with one eye, then the other. Her cheeks dimple.
– Thank you for a lovely trip, Mr. Baxter, she says. – It was a joy to meet you.

Mrs. Tupper twirls her parasol.

In his hand lie eight crinkled twenty-dollar bills.

His stomach leaps up into his throat, then down into his feet.

One hundred and sixty dollars.

He is going to dentistry school.

The train rolls on through Lake Louise, Field, Revelstoke, and finally Sicamous.

Punch and Judy detrain in Sicamous even though they're supposed to detrain in Vancouver. No sister waits for them at the platform.

Punch gives Baxter twenty-five cents.

Their Drawing Room compartment waits plush and ready for its next passengers. Warm.

In the passageway, the Doctor trips and touches the small of Baxter's back as he steadies himself, just for a second, his hand in the small of Baxter's back the way a stranger might steady himself, but the way a stranger likely wouldn't.

The train hauls to a stop at the terminal station, Vancouver. The passengers flood down the corridors and spurt and jostle out the doors. Twenty-five cents, fifty cents, thirty-five cents, one dollar, five cents. Fifty cents. Red Caps sweep forward to catch up suitcases and bags, hatboxes. They lurch and juggle trunks and suit-cases, one balances a birdcage.

Granny detrains, but Esme stays, clutching on to him. For his tip, Granny hands him back his copy of *The Scarab from Jupiter*.

A man in a striped suit strides toward Granny. He kisses her cheek. They contemplate each other in a moment of silence in the midst of the railway station clamour.

– I'm so tired, says Granny.

The man kisses her other cheek.

– How is she? he asks.

Granny draws a handkerchief out of her bag and wipes her eyes. She shakes her head.

Esme tucks herself behind Baxter's legs. The man in the striped suit reaches a hand out to Esme.

– Esme, he says. – It's Papa. Esme.

She shrinks away.

Baxter crouches down, gently holds her by her thin shoulders. – It's your papa, he says.

She frowns as he tries to stand up. She's grabbed his arm, she grabs for his neck, bumping his temple with the porcelain horse. He winces. Then he laughs because Esme's father and Granny are watching him.

– Listen, he says to Esme. – Would you like to keep my book? My *Scarab from Jupiter*? That way we can remember each other?

She begins to cry, her eyes raw and red, her nose soggy with tears, Rocky tucked up into her armpit.

He holds the book out to her. She weeps, her mouth downturned. She hiccups. She untucks the horse from her armpit and stands with it in both hands. She holds her horse out to him.

He takes the horse. She takes the book.

She traces the beetle on the cover with her finger, wraps her arms around the book, and hugs it tightly. He wraps his hands around the horse. He waves goodbye as her father gathers her up into his arms, her short gargoyle legs, she waves and waves and waves at Baxter until she and her father and grandmother are swallowed into the crowds, and her wild waving disappears. Baxter steps up into the car, his throat hurting, the little horse cradled in his hands.

Granny gave no tip at all. Maybe he will be fired anyway.

He helps more passengers descend, helps them transfer their bags from the train to the platform.

He helps Dr. Hubble with a bag although the Doctor's strong enough and capable enough to handle it on his own.

– Goodbye, says Dr. Hubble.

They stand, regarding each other, a flicker too long, a fraction too close.

– Nice to meet you, sir, says Baxter.

– Really nice to meet you too, sir, says the Doctor.

The Doctor curls a crumpled bill into Baxter's hand. Baxter steps back up into the train, opens his palm. A dollar bill, and a page ripped out of a diary. Written in pen on the page: *I would like to see you again*. An address in Montreal. Signed, *Jasper*.

He folds the page and slides it into the pocket where the postcard used to be. The doctor has dissolved into the crowd too, digested into the guts of the station.

Even though Baxter still has work and cleaning up to do in his car, he can already smell the rainy green of Vancouver. He has to bundle up all the dirty linen, mark all the lost and forgotten items into the Lost Article register.

He rings the buzzer on Compartment A's door. He knocks his knuckles on the wood. And when Andrew Swain doesn't answer, Baxter swings open the door, ready for a mess to end all messes.

Empty. The compartment dusted and scrubbed as clean as when Baxter first boarded the train days and days ago. The compartment lies still, as though on a brink.

Baxter collects trash. Strips down the berths. The cars snake into the Drake Street yards for servicing.

He steps off the car in his trim porter's hat and coat, his bag in his hand, his shoes bright, always bright. The dining car waiters and crew, the steward, the pantryman, the chef and his juniors, Stanley the engineer, the brakeman, the fireman, Templeton, Freckles, and Mad Mary disperse. Ferdinand steps down too, thumbs at a scuff on his bag as he waits for Baxter. Their heels click as they stride to catch up to Templeton and Freckles who travel the platform to the train office to collect their checks. Learn of their demerits or their firings. All of their shoes shine bright, the gold buttons on their jackets also gleam.

He has no idea what will happen to him, what complaints will rain down upon his head. At headquarters he waits his turn behind the other porters.

Two demerits for insolence to a passenger. They won't tell him which passenger. And he's charged for three missing towels.

He orders noodles at a Chinese restaurant.

Afterward, he lies down in a bunk bed surrounded by twelve snoring porters in their bunk beds, his eyes wide open.

He catches the comet tail of a dream, then Ferdinand, three bunks over, asks him if he'd like to go for breakfast. Barely speaking, they guzzle coffee, bite into biscuits, eggs, pork.

They exit the restaurant, stomachs packed.

– D'you know what's happened to Eugene Grady? asks Baxter. – Will he find another job?

– Oh, Eugene, says Ferdinand, his hands deep in his pockets. – One of his wives is a washwoman for disorderly houses. The other has a hair salon. They'll take care of him.

Grey, billowing clouds slip across the sky, the wind high.

Baxter pokes the dirt with his toe. He takes a breath before he speaks, but he has to know. He has to find out if someone knows.

– What about a fellow named Edwin Drew? You ever heard of him?

– Fella who's a Porter Instructor? asks Ferdinand. – Went to jail?

Baxter lifts off his cap with his left hand, runs his right hand over his hair, replaces the cap. He straightens his collar. He'll get his hair cut before tomorrow.

– That fella, says Ferdinand. – He put money down on a place in Montreal where he's going to open a nightclub, says Ferdinand, his coat snapping with the breeze. – He was smuggling liquor, you know.

Baxter starts to laugh. – I guess that's bad, Baxter says.

He laughs and laughs until he hiccups with laughter, and his stomach spasms from so much laughing.

– Very bad, says Ferdinand, laughing too, his mouth broad, his laugh deep. – What's so funny?

They both laugh. – Why! Are! We! Laughing! laughs Ferdinand.

Their laughs peter out.

– I guess I'll be going, says Baxter. He shakes Ferdinand's hand.

Except for a barber, he doesn't know where he'll go between now and tomorrow when he'll loiter in the station, waiting for a run.

Ferdinand says to him, – Do you want to come fly my kite with me?

Baxter can't tell if he's dreaming.

Ferdinand tells Baxter that his wife designed and made the kite, sewed it together with her seamstress's fingers.

Baxter blinks at the wind pummelling his face, not sleepy at all. The wind whips off his hat, and he has to chase it down the street.

– Yes! he shouts.

They find a grassy patch, and Baxter can't help smiling as he runs, his muscles joyous as they pump at full strength, proper strength, as his arms and legs splay and kick out, the wind swooping against his and Ferdinand's bodies. Both men laugh as they run, their mouths wide, the wind pushing and cajoling, their coats filling up and billowing like the clouds above them.

Baxter gallops, the kite in his arms, and when Ferdinand shouts at him to *Let go*, Baxter lets go. He marvels at the shining kite rising up, whipping back and forth, up and up into the cloudy sky.

NOTES

While I have done my very best to research and stick to the historical facts, and any historical errors are wholly mine, in the writing of this book I sometimes had to ascribe to what Kate Atkinson writes: 'sometimes to find the truth at the heart of a book a certain amount of reality falls by the wayside.'

The 'Want a Job?' image on page 8 is drawn from two ads in *The Crisis*, Nov. 1913, pp. 350–51.

The image of the layout of the train car on page 28 is from Gary W. Anderson's *Canadian Pacific's Trans-Canada Limited (1919–1930)*.

The line 'hearts will never be practical until they can be made unbreakable' is from the film *The Wizard of Oz* (1939).

'He twirled one too many times in front of his female cousins. He was the best twirler of all of them' is derived from a tweet written by Deborah Divine – Dan Levy's mom – where she comments on how Levy used to love to twirl as a child: 'Today I regret every single second of worry back in the uninformed 80's – wondering how the world was going to treat my brilliant little boy who loved to twirl. Little did I know that he was going to kick that old world's ass to the curb and create a brand new one.'

The phrase 'Make them drunker' comes from Jack Santino's book, *Miles of Smiles, Years of Struggle: Stories of Black Pullman Porters*.

The alleyway sex scene on page 195 is derived from a scene described in Steven Maynard's 'Six Nights in the Albert Lane, 1917.'

An excerpt from an earlier draft was published in *Canada and Beyond: A Journal of Canadian Literary and Cultural Studies*, Vol. 8, 2019.

ACKNOWLEDGEMENTS

Thank you to the brilliant, beloved people who read, marked up, reread, re-marked up, and listened in the dead of night and the dead of day: Nicole Markotić, Rosemary Nixon.

Thank you to Alana Wilcox for her editorial eyes that are as sharp as a mantis shrimp's, and her wicked brain that helped push me over the finish line. Thank you to everyone at Coach House Books.

Thank you to the people who helped spark this novel into being: Fred Wah, Cheryl Foggo, Don Bragg, John Harewood, Melanie Boyd.

Thank you to Saje Mathieu, Steven Maynard, and Wayde Compton for their historical expertise and advice.

Thank you for the important miscellaneous: Jess Nicol (my post-doctoral supervisor), Hollie Adams, Craig Lewington, Joanne Pohn, Heather Stirrup, Barb Hume, Jim Hume, Jonathan Ball, Carole Taylor, Brian Jansen, Dawn Bryan, George Chauncey, Shane Book, Kristine Stewart, Bethany Paul, Derrick Paul, Carly Stewart, Nancy Jo Cullen, Faye Halpern, Anthony Camara, Morgan Vanek, André Alexis, Jon Rozhon, Barb Levine, Melissa Wang Jackson, Erina Harris, Julia Gaunce, Sharon Brawn, Vivek Shraya, Cheryl Thompson, Stefania Forlini, Alice Zorn. My family (mostly alphabetical): Tonya, Friedrich, Hannah, Julien, Maya, Rose-Marie, Ulrich, Vanessa, Wendy, Coco, Brossy, Sido, Pushkin, Rio.

Thank you to Don Kirk, David Humphrey, and Honor Neve at the Cranbrook History Centre.

The following libraries and archives, and the staff who work there, were invaluable: the Archives of Manitoba, the University of Manitoba Archives and Special Collections, the Newberry Library Pullman Company Archives, the Exporail Canadian Railway Museum, Library and Archives Canada, the City of Vancouver Archives, UBC Library's

Chung Collection, the Calgary Police Services Archives, the Schomburg Center for Research in Black Culture.

The majority of the research for this book was made possible by a generous Insight Grant from the Social Sciences and Humanities Research Council (SSHRC).

Thank you again, as always, to Tonya Callaghan. Words cannot.

WORKS CONSULTED

Anderson, Garry W. *Canadian Pacific's Trans-Canada Limited* (1919–1930). 1990. Canadian Museum of Rail Travel, 1996.

Arnesen, Eric. *Brotherhoods of Colour: Black Railroad Workers and the Struggle for Equality*. Harvard University Press, 2002.

Beam, Joseph. *In the Life: A Black Gay Anthology*. 1986. Redbone Press, 2008.

Bird, J. Malcolm. *'Margery' the Medium*. Small, Maynard, & Co., 1925. HathiTrust.

Chauncey, George. *Gay New York: Gender, Urban Culture, and the Making of the Gay Male World 1890–1940*. Basic Books, 1994.

Compton, Wayde. *After Canaan: Essays on Race, Writing, and Region*. Arsenal Pulp Press, 2010.

Crichlow, Wesley. *Buller Men and Batty Bwoys: Hidden Men in Toronto and Halifax Black Communities*. University of Toronto Press, 1994.

Derickson, Alan. "'Asleep and Awake at the Same Time": Sleep Denial Among Pullman Porters.' *Labor: Studies in Working Class History*, Vol. 5, Issue 3, Fall 2008, pp. 13–44.

Foster, Cecil. *They Call Me George: The Untold Story of Black Train Porters and the Birth of Modern Canada*. Biblioasis, 2019.

Gairey, Harry. *A Black Man's Toronto 1914–1980: The Reminiscences of Harry Gairey*. Ed. Donna Hill. Multicultural History Society of Ontario, 1981.

Gardiner, James, and Montague Charles Glover. *A Class Apart: The Private Pictures of Montague Glover*. Serpent's Tail, 1992.

Grizzle, Stanley G. *My Name's Not George: The Story of the Brotherhood of Sleeping Car Porters in Canada: Personal Reminiscences of Stanley G. Grizzle*. Umbrella Press, 1998.

Hemphill, Essex. *Ceremonies: Prose and Poetry*. Plume, 1992.

Holderness, Herbert O. *The Reminiscences of a Pullman Conductor or Character Sketches of Life in a Pullman Car.* Chicago, 1901.

Hughes, Lyn. *An Anthology of Respect: The Pullman Porters National Historic Registry of African American Railroad Employees.* Hughes Peterson Publishing, 2007.

Jacob, Selwyn, dir. *The Road Taken.* National Film Board of Canada, 1996.

Kirvin, Johnnie F. *Hey Boy! Hey George: The Pullman Porter: A Memoir,* 2009.

Korinek, Valerie J. *Prairie Fairies: A History of Queer Communities and People in Western Canada, 1930–1985.* University of Toronto Press, 2018.

Kornweibel Jr., Theodore. *Railroads in the African American Experience: A Photographic Journey.* Johns Hopkins University Press, 2010.

Lorinc, John, et al. *The Ward: The Life and Loss of Toronto's First Immigrant Neighbourhood.* Coach House Books, 2015.

Maloney, Russell. 'Pullman Porter: Among Other Things, He Must Be a Practical Psychologist and a Minor Miracle Worker.' *Holiday,* November 1947.

Marlatt, Daphne, and Carole Itter. *Opening Doors: Vancouver's East End.* Sound Heritage, Vol. 8, Nos. 1 and 2, 1979.

Mathieu, Saje. *North of the Colour Line: Migration and Black Resistance in Canada, 1870–1955.* University of North Carolina Press, 2010.

Maynard, Steven. 'Six Nights in the Albert Lane, 1917.' *Any Other Way: How Toronto Got Queer.* Coach House Books, 2017, pp. 93–95.

———. 'Through a Hole in the Lavatory Wall: Homosexual Subcultures, Police Surveillance, and the Dialectics of Discovery, Toronto, 1890–1930.' *Journal of the History of Sexuality,* Vol. 5, No. 2, Oct. 1994, pp. 207–42.

———. '"Without Working?": Capitalism, Urban Culture and Gay History.' *Journal of Urban History*, Vol. 30, Issue 3, March 1, 2004, pp. 378–98.

McKissack, Patricia, and Frederick. *A Long Hard Journey: The Story of the Pullman Porter*. Walker and Co., 1989.

Nugent, Richard Bruce. 'Smoke, Lilies, and Jade.' *Fire!* Vol. 1, No. 1, 1926. HathiTrust.

Perata, David D. *Those Pullman Blues: An Oral History of the African American Railroad Attendant*. 1996. Madison Books, 1999.

The Pullman Porter. Issued by the Brotherhood of Sleeping Car Porters, 1927. HathiTrust.

Robertson, Beth A. *Science of the Séance: Transnational Networks and Gendered Bodies in the Study of Psychic Phenomena, 1918–40*. UBC Press, 2016.

Rogers, J. A. *From Superman to Man*, 1917. HathiTrust.

Santino, Jack. *Miles of Smiles, Years of Struggle: Stories of Black Pullman Porters*. University of Illinois Press, 1989.

Sarsfield, Mairuth. *No Crystal Stair*. 1997. Women's Press, 2004.

Swift, E. M., and C. S. Boyd. 'The Pullman Porter Looks at Life.' *The Psychoanalytic Review: A Journal Devoted to an Understanding of Human Conduct*. Vol. 15, Washington, DC, 1928. pp. 393–416.

Townsend, Robert, dir. *10,000 Black Men Named George*. Showtime Networks, 2002.

Tye, Larry. *Rising from the Rails: Pullman Porters and the Making of the Black Middle Class*. Henry Holt and Co., 2004.

Washington, Eric K. *Boss of the Grips: The Life of James H. Williams and the Red Caps of Grand Central Terminal*. Liveright, 2019.

Waugh, Thomas. *Hard to Imagine: Gay Male Eroticism in Photography and Film from Their Beginnings to Stonewall*. Columbia University Press, 1996.

Welsh, Joe, et al. *The Cars of Pullman*. Crestline Books, 2015.

Suzette Mayr is the author of the novels *Dr. Edith Vane and the Hares of Crawley Hall, Monoceros, Moon Honey, The Widows*, and *Venous Hum. The Widows* was shortlisted for the Commonwealth Writers' Prize for Best Book in the Canada-Caribbean region, and has been translated into German. *Moon Honey* was shortlisted for the Writers' Guild of Alberta's Best First Book and Best Novel Awards. *Monoceros* won the ReLit Award, the City of Calgary W. O. Mitchell Book Prize, was longlisted for the 2011 Giller Prize, and shortlisted for a Ferro-Grumley Award for LGBT Fiction, and the Georges Bugnet Award for Fiction. She and her partner live in a house in Calgary across the street from a park teeming with coyotes.

Typeset in Arno and Aviano Sans.

Coach House is on the traditional territory of many nations, including the Mississaugas of the Credit, the Anishnabeg, the Chippewa, the Haudenosaunee, and the Wendat peoples, and is now home to many diverse First Nations, Inuit, and Métis peoples. We acknowledge that Toronto is covered by Treaty 13 with the Mississaugas of the Credit. We are grateful to live and work on this land.

Edited by Alana Wilcox
Cover design by Ingrid Paulson, cover art *Unapologetically William* by Janet Hill
Interior design by Crystal Sikma
Author photo by Tonya Callaghan

Coach House Books
80 bpNichol Lane
Toronto ON M5S 3J4
Canada

416 979 2217
800 367 6360

mail@chbooks.com
www.chbooks.com